The Gryphon and His Thief

by

Karen Michelle Nutt

The Gryphon and His Thief

COPYRIGHT © 2022 by Karen Michelle Nutt

Contact Information: info@thewildrosepress.com

Cover Art by *Kristian Norris*

The Wild Rose Press, Inc.
PO Box 708
Adams Basin, NY 14410-0708
Visit us at www.thewildrosepress.com

Publishing History
First Edition, 2022
Trade Paperback ISBN 978-1-5092-4177-4
Digital ISBN 978-1-5092-4178-1

Published in the United States of America

Fearing she'd spring to life and bolt again, he soared to his feet and strode toward her, but she lay unmoving with only the rise and fall of her chest to tell him she still lived.

"Unfortunate for you, my dear sweet thief," he murmured. Her unconscious state made slicing her neck and taking back what belonged to the museum that much easier. He crouched down next to her and released his talons from his fingertips with a slight shift.

"Ah…soooo…nice," the thief murmured, her voice like a sweet melody to his ears.

He frowned and stared at her, his clawed hand ready to slash, but he didn't act. Instead, he found himself mesmerized as her tongue slipped out to moisten those pink lips of hers. He thought she would awaken, but then she shifted her bottom and settled as she curled on her side.

He retracted his claws. Curiosity got the better of him, and he had to behold the thief's true features. He reached for the ski mask and yanked it off her head. Waves of ginger strands tumbled out like autumn arriving by storm and summer being left behind by the raging winds.

He blinked in surprise, and his blood pounded in his temples as he absorbed her every feature, features he knew as well as his own. "Callista?" he breathed the name, though it took all the air from him as if she sucker punched him.

The thief…this woman couldn't be his lady wife.

Praise for The Gryphon and His Thief

"The plot moves along at a cracking pace and the fantasy elements are not over played. They are, in fact, very believable." ~Susan Day, Author/Blogger Astro's Adventures

"Nutt's writing is crisp, fast, and engaging. She makes fantasy come alive with this modern-day tale in a totally believable way. Calli is loyal and sincere. Darrien is a true hero and Isa is absolutely delicious as the villain." ~Stephanie Burkhart, Bestselling Author

Dedication

To my readers! Without you, my tales would be forgotten. You rock!

Acknowledgments

Special thanks to Cathy for always reading my rough drafts. A million thanks and more for all your thoughts and suggestions. You are the best!

Chapter One

Calli Angelis glanced around the empty parking lot with only the light from the moon to illuminate the empty car spaces. Bushes and fairy duster shrubs with their pink and red flowers decorated the vast Arizona desert behind it, along with rocks and gravel. The weather proved mild for October, and sage scented the air with aromatic notes of earth and sunlight on varnished desert rock.

She dressed for the occasion with dark clothing, hiking boots, and a ski mask, making sure her ginger hair stayed hidden and didn't flap in the wind like a fiery warning flag.

Confirming she was indeed the only one lurking around the Museum of Cursed Antiquities, she fished out her tools of the trade attached to her tool belt and went to work on the lock. The museum was more like a glorified warehouse, rustic and foreboding if anyone cared for her opinion.

With her forefinger and thumb, she worked the tool and listened for the click. To think she almost hadn't taken this job. Professor Leander had struck her as a little on the weird side, but in the end, who was she to judge as long as her offshore bank account had multiple zeroes behind a grand number.

Since her father's passing less than six months ago, she'd been on her own. Cancer was a real bitch. Her father had been tough as nails, but the disease had won anyway. So when Professor Leander offered her a way out of a pile of bills and creditors who kept calling the house, she ignored the niggling in the back of her mind and signed on to do the job.

It had taken her over a month to trace where the artifact had been taken once it had been unearthed at a location just north of the Delphi Archeological site in Greece. Professor Leander, or rather the Leander Corporation, funded the dig with guards on duty at all hours, but still someone had infiltrated the compound and stole the item right under everyone's noses. Probably an inside job but any practiced thief could manage such a feat. Nothing proved positively fortified in her book.

The resounding click of the lock made her smile, and she reached for the door handle with confidence.

Earlier today she'd cased the place. Not one person visited, but the curator appeared to be a nerdy looking guy who sipped tea all day while he kept his nose buried in a book. Casing the place for hours proved tiresome, and she must have dozed for a second. She hadn't seen the guy leave the building, but for the last half hour, the lights remained off and the place appeared as quiet as a tomb. If she had more time, she'd wait another day, stake it out again, and this time make sure she had enough caffeine in her system to keep alert. Unfortunately, she didn't have the luxury. The October 31st deadline she agreed to loomed. If she didn't place the item in Professor Leander's hands, the second installment promised to her for her troubles would be forfeited.

Her time line was already cutting it short, but she still had plenty of time to deliver it to the professor tomorrow, if she nabbed the item tonight. Then next she'd head to New Orleans for some rest and relaxation… Well, more like party hardy at a costume ball her cousin Mick was throwing for Halloween. The man knew how to rock and roll.

Luckily, the museum didn't possess an alarm system, so she didn't have to worry about disarming it. "In and out," she murmured. "Easy-peasy." Her hand slipped the flashlight from her tool belt, and she clicked the button. Light illuminated the place, highlighting the items in a grotesque glow, making the place appear more like a house of horrors than a museum. "Museum of Cursed Antiquities," she reminded herself. With this view, she could well imagine the title to be true. Everything seemed to be catalogued in sections in a semblance of order. Dolls to the left of her, some small, some as tall as a toddler, all with various hair styles from bald to curly, and hair color ranging from dark to light.

"What the heck…" Had the one with the sailor hat winked at her? She cringed at the thought and hurried on down the path. Furniture came next, chairs, sofas, lamps…then torture devices. She passed by a guillotine that stood in the corner on the right. The sign stated: Haunted by the headless Lady Marie Devull. Well, really now. The woman was probably looking for her head. No wonder she haunted the darn thing.

Her fingers subconsciously caressed the chrysoprase amulet she wore on a silver chain around her neck. Her father claimed the apple green and slightly fluorescent stone was a thief's stone used in ancient times to protect the person from being hanged or…beheaded. In this century, hopefully it warded off being arrested too.

She strode past a curio filled with items that were supposedly haunted or cursed by their previous owners—gloves, photographs, brooches—to name a few. At the end of the aisle, Sarcophagi stood in a row, like soldiers guarding over the damned. All were decorated with painted representations of the deceased—or so she imagined—sightless black eyes and ghastly grins. "I take it your curse is being ugly buggers." She stifled a laugh and pursed her lips. She shouldn't make fun of the dead, and most assuredly not in here.

To the right was another room, the sign above stated Rocks, Minerals, Jewels, and Stones. "Exactly what I was looking for," she murmured. As long as the curator documented and logged the new arrival, the stone should be in there.

She took a step into the room only to come up short as the light from the flashlight landed on glowing eyes. "Holy—" the curse stuck in her throat as she stumbled back. Her heart had surely decided to lodge itself in her throat, but she forced herself to take a deep gulping breath and let it out again.

"Get a grip," she murmured and shone the light in the direction of the glowing eyes to reveal the threat as an enormous statue of a mythical beast with the body, tail, and back legs of a lion and the head, talons, and wings of an eagle. It was both fierce and majestic with eyes made of precious stones—or so she assumed with the way the light reflected off of them. She shone the flashlight at the base, looking for a card stating why it stood in the museum, but couldn't locate one. "Mr. Gryphon, I'm curious, why are you here?" She didn't know much about the creatures, but a portrait of a gryphon hung in her father's study… her study now. She never had the heart to change the décor and truthfully, she'd always liked the painting.

Her hand smoothed over the flank of the statue, not fearing she'd leave fingerprints since black leather gloves were a thief's fashion statement. "You are a beauty." She sighed with regret. "Sorry, Big Boy, I'm on a job. Can't stop to chat." She patted the creature and moved toward the glass case located a few feet behind it. A long-forgotten teacup sat on top, half filled, a slice of lemon resting on the saucer. She removed the cup, placing it on the ground at her feet. Her gaze then shifted over each item in the case, skimming the information listed on the cards. She had in mind to leave the curator a thank you note for being so meticulous in cataloging the artifacts.

Her gaze landed on the item she'd come to retrieve with an index card placed beneath it, but the info about the piece hadn't been typed on it yet. There was only the name of the item and a number, probably a catalog number since all the other exhibits possessed one too.

Her hand smoothed along the lip of the case, feeling for the release mechanism. "There you are," she murmured and pressed the lever. The top opened with ease. She shook her head wondering why the owner was so trusting. No alarm system, no locks on the curios… Heck, she was surprised the front door hadn't been left wide open.

"Yeah, enter at your own risk." Guess there wasn't a high demand on cursed objects. She slid the case open and reached for the egg-shaped stone. Once she had the stone in her grasp, she carefully closed the glass top.

She stared at the item with curiosity. It wasn't anything special to look at and if she'd seen it on the ground, it wouldn't be a stone she'd snatch up as a treasure. Black as ebony and smooth to the touch, it sat in the palm of her hand. No color change, no vibration but heat radiated through her glove. Not an unpleasant sensation, and on a cold night it might be a welcomed item stashed in a pocket. Her eyebrows furrowed, as she wondered what misfortune it harbored, and if picking it up could somehow trigger the curse to respond.

She turned it over in her hand to inspect it further then rolled her eyes at the absurdity of her line of questioning. "Curses…yeah, right," but she didn't completely dismiss the idea an object could be cursed. Her family had their share of superstitions passed down through the generations and it was hard to shake them off as being silly folklore. Besides, if the stone proved truly cursed, it couldn't just rub off on a person by touching it. Professor Leander had obviously handled the item at the dig site with no worries.

She slipped the stone in the pouch secured at her waist, before closing the lid to the case and returning the teacup to its rightful resting spot on the glass counter. She then turned to leave, retracing her steps but came up short when her flashlight illuminated a wide-open path. "Where in the heck is the gryphon?" she said aloud. She really had to stop talking to herself.

The statue stood over six feet tall and had to weigh a ton. It would be difficult to miss, let alone forget where it stood in the room.

With a shake of her head, she dismissed her judgement. The shadows in the dark room must have

6

confused her. She shifted the flashlight, letting the light shine around the area in a slow arc. Expecting to find the creature standing as regal and unmoving as she'd left it, she shifted her attention to every shadow and even up toward the rafters. "Oh come now. It couldn't have taken flight." It wasn't there.

Of course not. There wasn't room for it to fly— even if it could, she reminded herself. It was a sculpture not a living, breathing creature, and yet her explanation didn't prevent the fine hairs on the back of her neck from rising to attention.

The place was cluttered with artifacts. She'd merely miscalculated where it had stood. The pouch still hung at her side. She patted it. It was what she came for. There was no need to debate why her psyche conjured a gryphon statue. She turned her light in a wide circle one more time. There obviously wasn't one.

She hurried out of the room at a jog toward the front of the museum, only to slide to a halt as she caught sight of something immersed in shadows, blocking the front entrance.

"It can't be," she said, her voice a hoarse whisper. Angling her light on the object ahead, the gryphon stood tall and fierce as if glaring directly at her.

Her tongue slipped out, and she licked her suddenly dry lips. How in the world had the statue moved from the back room to here? The neat magic trick proved, at the very least, amazing. Then her gaze met its eyes and the damned thing blinked.

"Holy… What the…" Both exclamations stopped unfinished as she stumbled back and rammed her hip into the corner of one of the glass tables covered with cursed items. "Crap." All she needed was to break something. "Get a grip," she warned herself. The gryphon didn't blink his eyes. Yep, and it didn't fly from the back room and station itself at the door, either. She gulped and leveled the beam of the flashlight on the statue once more. Only what stood there now was a man, a large man with dark hair, a beard neat and trim…and eyes that glowed like the gryphon's eyes had.

"You cannot take the item from the museum," the man's deep voice boomed with authority meant to intimidate, and his words were flavored with a Greek accent. "You must return it immediately," he finished the threat. Sure there had been no threat voiced, but she all but heard the 'or else' just as clearly as if the words had been spoken.

"Who are you?" she countered, even though she had no right to inquire. Obviously, this man must be the night guardsman. Her gaze slid over his attire and frowned. He wore garments she'd only seen painted on Greek vases and paintings—an intricately designed tunic, a dark colored cloak, and gold sandals adorned his feet. Her one eyebrow lifted. Perhaps he was a thief who liked theatrics. She had an uncle who liked to dress like a caped superhero when he went on his jobs.

She straightened her back and met the guy's gaze head on. "I think you need to leave, or I'll call the cops." She pulled out her cell phone and lit up the screen to prove her point. The guy didn't have to know she was bluffing. She didn't want the cops here anymore than he probably did.

He didn't quite react the way she thought he would. Oh no, he had the audacity to laugh, a deep guttural laugh. "You amuse me human woman," he told

8

her.

"Human woman?" Okay, this nut-job was off his meds. "Fine, you stay here, and this human woman will say good evening. It's been a long day. I need to head back to my spaceship before E.T. calls home and tells Mom and Dad I'm late."

The man's brows furrowed, deep creases marring his forehead. Maybe she loaded on the crapola a little thick. It was best to end this conversation and get out of Africa—as her father would say—and make like a cheetah on the hunt. She took a few cautious steps toward the front door.

"You will halt," he demanded with his palm up as if his stance alone could stop her.

Well, yep it did, for a full three seconds. She knew some self-defense moves, but this guy was built like he lifted weights in his sleep just so his bulk didn't decrease in the middle of the night. It didn't appear like the front door was an option, but... her gaze latched onto the window next to it. "Oh, hell." She charged and prayed this old building hadn't been refurbished with safety glass. Otherwise, this stunt was really going to hurt.

Chapter Two

Darrien stared in disbelief at the thief wearing a knit hat that covered her hair and most of her face. However, despite the attempt at a disguise, there was no mistaking the thief's gender as female even before she spoke. Lovely green eyes with thick lashes peered at him over a petite nose, and her luscious lips demanded him to comply. If the features and the voice hadn't given her gender away, the curves her dark fitting outfit displayed, certainly would have.

He knew for a fact his stance intimidated, but she faced him with courage and the determination of a warrior. Either she was mad, or braver than she ought to be. In the next second, he had his answer. Madness truly plagued her.

His eyes widened in horror as she raced toward the window beside the door with its rectangular shape and framed in wood. It wasn't nearly wide enough to pull such a stunt as she intended. He cursed in the language of his youth, a dialect similar to the Greeks' language of ancient time, but more guttural. She would surely kill herself or, at the very least, cause some considerable damage to her person. She was human, but he sensed there was more to her, not a demigod, but something more powerful than a mere mortal. It proved a shame to waste such a life, but he would have to end it. He could not allow her to take one of the cursed items out of the museum. As guardian, thievery on his watch meant a sure death to the culprit. Maybe he should let her crash into the glass and save him the trouble. She'd most likely break her neck or sever an artery, but then the fool woman may surprise him further and survive. No, he must stop her now.

His magic curled around him, and he took the form of ether, reappearing in front of the woman, but she proved quick on her feet and maneuvered around him. With one last effort, his hand snaked out to clasp her wrist. She swung with her other hand, and something sliced into his flesh. The sharp pain made his grip falter when she yanked her arm, leaving him holding only her glove. Her body propelled through the window.

She'd raised her arms to shield her face as the glass shattered, and her scream pierced his eardrum, the sound as deafening as screeching gargoyles when they mated. Covering his ears reflexively until silence blessed the heavens, then he lowered his hands and stared at the window now sporting a jagged glass hole. He strode toward it, expecting to find her sprawled on the ground in a heap of blood and shards, but the little thief hadn't even paused as she landed. His gaze caught sight of her sprinting around the side of the building. Befuddled, he pondered over how she managed to pull off the elaborate feat.

Finally, he snapped into action and stepped over the ledge, the glass crunching beneath his sandals. Once outside he changed forms and took flight as the creature men feared, both eagle and lion, fierce and unrelenting when pursuing a thief. This woman proved not to be a coward. She was brave or foolhardy but worthy of the chase. His wings flapped, one, two, three times, the wind guiding him to the spot above her. She glanced up anticipating his intent with keen eyes of her own. As he dove at her with his talons stretched and readied to tear, she whirled around at the same time and released the weapon she wielded in her hand. Her dagger flew straight and true like an arrow meant to slay a beast on a hunt. His eyes widened in admiration at her skill, and at the last millisecond, he switched shapes again, disappearing into the wind in his ether form. The dagger harmlessly passed through him. Neatly avoiding being slain, but unable to materialize once more quickly enough, she had jumped in her vehicle and driven away as if the wind itself gave the metal beast flight.

He took to the air and went after her, keeping pace but not attacking as he thought of another plan. His direct approach hadn't worked. He needed to change tactics to catch this wily thief. He kept pace high above and directly over her sedan so she could not pinpoint his pursuit from her vehicle.

It was still hours before the sun would rise, and he had plenty of time before he needed to return to the museum. One hour after sunrise he would once again turn to stone, a curse he must endure for the crime he committed. He would be forever a guardsman for the Museum of Cursed Antiquities. No matter where the artifacts found a home through the centuries—be it overseas, in the States, or any place the founders, as he called them, saw fit to place the items—he was at their mercy. He could awaken tomorrow and find they'd moved the museum yet again.

In truth, it didn't matter where he guarded. His curse didn't allow him to venture far from the artifacts, unless someone dared to steal an object. Then his beastie nature would take over. He would hunt the thief with little trouble. Numerous men, brave and brilliant had tried, and still they'd failed. It took no more than one evening to track them and end their lives before returning the object to its rightful berth in the museum. Those men were bloody fools, the lot of them, to go up against a gryphon.

Only, the thief tonight had been a woman. He sighed heavily. It did not matter, he thought with determination. The end result would be the same. She'd stolen a stone that housed the power of an evil Necromancer. If such an item fell into the wrong hands, a new meaning to this century's term "hell on earth" would ensue.

In a few days, the veil between life and death would be at its weakest. The one wielding the stone would be able to call on the dead with ease and bend them to their will. Charon, the ferryman, who ferried the dead to Hades, would not be able to deny such a request. He would be forced to bring the souls through the veil one by one.

This could not happen. If the dead walked among the living, they would eventually feed off of them. They would crave the energy that makes the living thrive. No, he could not allow the thief to accomplish such a goal.

The thief's vehicle pulled into the parking lot of a motel where a sign flashed "vacancy" in red on the marquee. Another sign on a door to the main building overlooked the street and directed customers to check in. The rooms were located adjacent to it. The one-story units had different color doors, but all had gold numbers nailed to the center, ranging from one to twenty. The thief pulled into a car slot in front of a room with a dark green door marked number seven. By the look of the parking lot there was possibly only one other room rented for the night, which made his job much easier. If the occupant decided to be a good, law-abiding citizen, he'd take him out too.

He meant to perch on the roof of the building and keep to the shadows of the overhanging tree, but at the last second he landed on the earth behind the shrubbery. His location, opposite where the thief parked, provide a better view of her next move, without him being too obvious—once he changed into his human form.

He would have preferred the clothing he remembered from his youth. Instead, he fashioned himself in the current style of this era. He glanced down and smoothed his hand over the *I Love Rock and Roll* T-shirt. The worn blue jeans were comfortable, but then he frowned when his gaze landed on his bare feet. In the next second, he visualized covering them with snakeskin boots and then nodded in approval. Crouching low behind the shrubbery, he waited to make his next move.

The woman stepped out of her sedan and hurried toward a room. Her hands shook as she tried to manage the keycard into the lock mechanism and ended up dropping it in the bushes next to the walkway. It took her a few seconds to retrieve it, giving him a nice view of her shapely bottom. His lips curved before he stopped himself and was surprised at where his thoughts had ventured. He had not admired a woman in a long time and the odd sensation left him unnerved. He rolled his eyes in annoyance and shook off his moment of weakness. He didn't have time for fanciful thoughts. He refocused and forced himself to concentrate on the thief's actions and not her comely attributes.

Once she had the keycard in her hand, he made his move, materializing beside her as she disengaged the lock to her door. She gasped and stepped back as if to flee, but he proved quicker and his hand snaked out, grabbing her wrist. He'd not make the same mistake twice and have her slip out of his grip, leaving him with only a glove for his trouble. The skin-to-skin contact sparked a current of electricity, a jolt worthy of Zeus' warning bolts, and by the heavens those stung.

They flew apart from the zap of energy and he slammed into the vending machine, sparking it to life and sending candy bars and chips dropping into the bin for easy access. The thief bounced against her vehicle, fell to the ground, and hit her head against the bumper on the way down, knocking her unconscious.

Fearing she'd spring to life and bolt again, he soared to his feet and strode toward her, but she lay unmoving with only the rise and fall of her chest to tell him she still lived.

"Unfortunate for you, my dear sweet thief," he murmured. Her unconscious state made slicing her neck and taking back what belonged to the museum that much easier. He crouched down next to her and released his talons from his fingertips with a slight shift.

"Ah…soooo…nice," the thief murmured, her voice like a sweet melody to his ears.

He frowned and stared at her, his clawed hand ready to slash, but he didn't act. Instead, he found himself mesmerized as her tongue slipped out to moisten those pink lips of hers. He thought she would awaken, but then she shifted her bottom and scttled as she curled on her side.

He retracted his claws. Curiosity got the better of him, and he had to behold the thief's true features. He reached for the ski mask and yanked it off her head. Waves of ginger strands tumbled out like autumn arriving by storm and summer being left behind by the raging winds.

He blinked in surprise, and his blood pounded in his temples as he absorbed her every feature, features he knew as well as his own. "Callista?" he breathed the name, though it took all the air from him, as if she'd sucker punched him.

The thief...this woman couldn't be his lady wife. She died centuries ago because he had not protected her. His failure had been the reason he'd been cursed, and yet he knew the woman at his feet was indeed his beloved. The shape of her eyes, the upturn of her nose and the lips...those kissable lips. How had he not seen it, even with the ridiculous disguise she'd worn?

Her groans alerted his attention to the situation at hand. She'd been hurt, and though she was strong, she'd hit her head and such an injury could prove fatal.

He scooped her into his arms with care and headed for her room before they drew unwanted attention. Once inside, he closed the door behind him with a kick of his boot and strode over to the bed, placing her gently on top of the covers. His hand brushed a wayward strand from her face, and she stirred, leaning toward his caress as if she sought his touch. No fiery spark, but he could still feel the energy pulsing between them as her cheek touched his palm.

His plans to eliminate her had taken a sharp turn. "Ah Callista, what am I to do now?" His guardsman's duties bade him to protect the cursed treasures at all cost. "…all costs," he murmured then shook his head. He could not harm Callista. Not when he'd been waiting all these centuries for her soul to be reborn to this world. No, he must convince her to return the stone on her own accord. It would be the only way to appease the beastie that raged inside of him.

His gaze slid over her features, so calm and relaxed in slumber, but he knew once she awakened, he would be faced with the warrior. Convincing her to do the right thing would prove to be his greatest challenge yet.

Chapter Three

Calli groaned as she came back to the world of the living. The constant throb at the back of her skull made her world seem off centered. She blinked and sat up, but the sudden movement proved to be a big mistake. A really big mistake. Her hand went to the side of her head as if she could stop her heartbeat from trying to settle in her eardrum. "What happened?" she asked, not expecting an answer.

"You are safe," a deep voice said, which in no way made her feel safe in the least. She bit off the urge to scream when she caught sight of a man lurking in the shadows.

Scrambling off the bed, she went for her dagger that should have been strapped to her belt. She realized too late she'd lost it when she threw it at the gryphon when he tried to eat her for a snack. She blinked—hard. Yep, that statement—though said to herself—definitely sounded like she lost her marbles, and the way her head pounded like jackhammers had taken up residence in her brain, convinced her the statement held merit.

She may have lost her dagger, but she'd been trained to improvise. Out of the corner of her eye, she caught sight of the phone sitting on the nightstand, black, push button and heavy. She grabbed it with the receiver in one hand and the base in the other. "Who are you and what are you doing in my room? Answer quick or I'm going to go all Nicky Santoro on your head."

She'd seen Casino and the phone treatment. Yep, considerable damage could be inflicted with a phone. She gripped the receiver and shook it in his direction for emphasis on her threat.

The man carefully stepped away from the shadows, revealing his features—rugged jaw, sharp planes, and high cheekbones.

"You!" Her word accused and condemned all in one roll of the tongue. How did the man from the museum find her?

Only seconds had ticked by as her brain played catch-up on the details of the night's events. When it did, it all came flooding back to her in Tsunami fashion. Stealing the stone... Greek god confronted her... gryphon attack in the parking ... Then a man grabbed her at the motel... Electric shock... She teetered on her feet as waves of emotions crashed down on her with each vision. Adrenaline rush... Attraction... Fear...

The man started toward her. One then two steps before she focused. "Don't come any closer. I swear..." She shook the phone at him. He halted his steps and held up his hands in surrender, which was kind of funny since he was in her room uninvited, and she was pretty sure he'd been the one to zap her into oblivion.

She needed to sit down, and her rump landed on the nightstand behind her. She planned on staying put until the room stopped its infernal spin cycle. "Who are you?" she demanded as she sized him up. His features took a second or two to come into focus. What she really wanted to ask him was: What are you? Because no normal human could materialize out of nowhere and zap a person with his bare hand. But hey, she could go with a name first. At least until she was steady on her feet and could put up a good fight—if things went down that way.

"Darrien," he said and bowed his head.

"Hmm… Darrien, no last name? Just Darrien, like you're a rock star or something." Her eyes shifted to his *I love Rock and Roll* T-shirt logo and her brows lifted in question. Maybe he really was in a band when he wasn't hanging out at museums and training gryphons to attack innocent bystanders. Well, not so innocent, but—she really needed to stop with the crazy scenarios.

"Callista, we must talk," he said. "I am not sure—"

"Who's Callista?" she questioned, interrupting him before he took this further.

"You don't remember me, do you?" he asked. She could see a battle going on inside him as if he couldn't comprehend why she didn't know him.

Yeah, confusion seemed to be catchy tonight. Well, it ended here. "For your information, *crazier-than-the-mad-hatter-on-a-good-day*, my name is Calli. So you have the wrong girl if you think I'm this Callista chick."

He tilted his head to the side, keeping his calm, and she might have believed he accomplished the feat, but then his eyes glowed like golden fire. "You truly do not remember me then?" he asked again.

She was still hung up on his eyes changing colors, and it took her a moment to realize he asked her a question. "No, whack-job, I don't know you. Unless you believed our introduction at the museum was a start of a beautiful friendship."

His lips pursed and his nose flared, probably due to the name-calling. Maybe she should give that a rest. She had no idea what she was dealing with, but if the man thought it was okay to taser her, it couldn't be good. She frowned as she remembered him coming upon her outside the motel room. She never saw a taser, and she could have sworn he grabbed her with his bare hand before the jolt zapped them apart. If that wasn't freaky enough, the special effects back at the museum proved more than she wanted to handle. God, she wished her head would stop pounding so she could think clearly.

She licked her dry lips and tried to think of a way out of the situation without ticking off the big guy. "Are you a magician or something? 'Cause the whole gryphon statue appearing and disappearing was kinda cool." Creepy also, but she kept that piece of information to herself.

There had to be an explanation to the weird experience. The statue moving around the museum was nothing compared to a friggin' gryphon swooping down from the heavens and attacking her. Her gaze met his and she blinked just to make sure she wasn't imagining what she was seeing. "Could you stop doing that…uh…" she pointed at him, "thingy you're doing with your eyes?"

His eyebrows furrowed over the bridge of his nose, and making him appear adorable when concern marred his expression. Dangerous and vulnerable all in one, she thought then shook her head. The guy may have the looks, but he wasn't playing with a full deck. Her gaze traveled down the length of him, admiring but also wondering when he had time to change his Greek mythology costume to his cool hang-low-on-the-hips jeans. How long had she been unconscious?.

"What is it I am doing?" he asked. "I assure you it

is not intentional."

It took her a moment to realize what he was talking about. Oh yeah… "Your eyes… They're glowing."

His lips curved, and that wasn't a bad look on him either. "It cannot be helped. It is the beastie, you see. It tries to dominate and is fueled by my emotions."

Did she really want to know what he meant by the beastie? It seemed she did when her next question slipped from her lips before she could think better of it. "The beastie?" she asked.

"Come now, Callista—"

"My name is Calli," she interrupted. She in no way was going to have him believe she was some chick he'd been involved with in the past.

"Calli," he said the name as if he were trying it out. He nodded then, as if his nutty messed up brain could handle the name change. "Calli, you spoke of seeing a gryphon." He met her gaze with those strange colored eyes, both bronze and gold. "The beastie and I are one and the same."

"Holy…" she stuttered. Truly there were no words, and as crazy as his statement seemed, she believed him.

Chapter Four

Darrien stood still and waited for what he told her to sink in. Any false moves would result in—what did she call it? Ah yes, she'd go all Nicky Santoro on his head. He didn't know what that entailed, but he had a good idea he wouldn't like such a treatment.

"You're a gryphon?" she more or less condemned rather than asked the question as her voice raised a few octaves in the telling. He usually liked the cadence of her voice, but not now when it made him feel bloody awful. "The very gryphon that tried to rip me to shreds?"

He nodded with a long, frustrated sigh. "Yes." There was no reason to pretend otherwise.

She blinked and her long lashes fluttered to rest on the tender flesh above her cheekbone like tiny butterflies of beautiful reddish brown. When she opened her eyes once more, those lovely eyes that were the color of moss and rimmed with a shade worthy of the sun's rays stared back at him. Or so he remembered and dreamt of often. It had been a very long time since he'd seen the sun...felt it on his face.

"So why am I not dead?" she asked, and her voice caught in her throat on a horrified whisper.

"You still live because of who you are to me."

She opened her mouth to say something, and he was sure it would be to the contrary, but her lips closed firmly, probably realizing how foolish such a denial would be. She most definitely didn't remember him or her past life. Perhaps it was his curse to be burdened so. His beloved thieved for a living, and his nature thrived on eliminating such talents. "If you put down your weapon," he told her, "I will explain."

"My weapon?" She glanced at the phone as if she just realized she still gripped it.

"Truly, such a weapon would be useless against me," he said, speaking the truth. Her gaze riveted to his, the gold of her eyes burning like fire. He raised his hands in surrender. "I do not wish to harm you. On my honor, I promise, you shall be safe this night." He could not in truth promise her more. Her safety depended on her relinquishing the stone. He had a hunch, his little thief wouldn't be forthcoming in handing it over, and he had already searched her person and had rummaged through her vehicle. He had not found the cursed item. She'd somehow managed to hide it somewhere between the museum and here, and he meant to find out where.

She placed the phone beside her on the nightstand, without taking her gaze off his. "Go on, spin your tale… Gryphon."

Where did one begin such a tale when she looked upon him as if lies, and naught else, flew off his tongue? To convince her otherwise would prove a challenge at best.

"Well?" Her tone indicated she was losing patience as the seconds ticked by. He must make his case now or forfeit the chance.

"You were my soul mate in another life," he blurted out and wondered at his lack of finesse.

She harrumphed. "No such thing, but please go on. Like most, I enjoy a good fairy tale."

He chose to ignore her sarcasm. He could not change her mind on what she believed, but perhaps if he told her the story, their story, she would at least consider his side. "Our love was thwarted by Isa, a jealous woman who believed I cared for her when I had not given her such attention."

"I just bet," she murmured.

"I love you, Callista." He could not keep the hurt from his voice. "My love is true and always has been, but you mock it." For a moment, their eyes met and maybe she witnessed the truth in his gaze for she lost her hostile stance.

"I'm sorry," she told him, and he believed she meant it. "I have no right to belittle your feelings for someone you care about."

After a pause, he nodded. "Apology accepted." He could not force her to remember their affection and did not correct her. He didn't just love someone. He loved her.

"But you must understand," she began as if she read his mind, "I am not this Callista. I don't remember you or the love you claim we shared. I'm Calli Marie Angelis. Calli is not short for Callista and never has been."

His gaze swept over her lovely features he remembered so well, and yet, there were differences too. Determination and spunk lit the features when Callista had not a temper at all, but she could be fierce if pushed, and perhaps in this, Calli and his beloved shared the trait. "Do you not feel anything for me?" he asked. "No spark at all of remembrance?"

"Great choice of words, Gryphon. Other than the jolt earlier when you touched me, no."

He lifted his hand and stared at his palm. Why had their first touch been so explosive?

"I don't remember you." Her voice drew his attention and he let his arm fall to his side. "I'm sorry, but I don't," she continued to insist. He wondered if it was for her benefit or his.

"Look at me," he told her. "Open your mind and try."

"Uh… Well," she cleared her throat and for a moment her eyes seemed to drink him in like a woman who had thirsted for a long time. "You're good looking and all…a bit intense, but if circumstances were different, I might have asked you out for a coffee." She nodded as her gaze slid from his face and lower then back up again. He had the urge to cover himself from her smoldering assessment.

"You undress me with your eyes," he told her, not sure if he should be offended or flattered at her wanton gaze.

Her chuckle rendered his pondering mute. "Wasn't I supposed to be the love of your life?" she asked. "I'm assuming we were intimate then." Her gaze slid over him again with meaning.

His brows lifted. "You do mock me still."

She rolled her eyes. "Get over yourself. Let's pretend I believe your little story here. So, we were star-crossed lovers in some past life, but this is the here and now and I have a life, a good one, and I don't see flying monkeys joining the mix."

"Flying monkeys?" He understood her words, but the meaning to them seemed to have been lost.

"You don't watch much TV locked up in the museum, do you?" She pushed away from the

26

nightstand and strode to the door. She opened it and turned toward him expectantly. "This is your cue to go."

She thought to dismiss him this readily. He flitted like the wind to her, slamming the door shut, and backing her up against it. His gaze met hers, flashing with a mix of excitement and fear. "We are not finished." He stepped closer to her, making it difficult for her to move around him.

"Step away," she warned with her hand to his chest, but she didn't push him away.

The heaven above, she was all soft curves and... she had a lethal left hook.

"Ouch!" He grabbed her arms and pinned them above her head. Big mistake. The woman moved faster than a panther and proved just as deadly. She slammed her head into his. He blinked and focused. "Stop it this instant, I say." This won him a swift kick to his shin.

Playing nice was over. Still holding her hands above her head and using his thighs to keep her from kicking him again, lest he find his nether parts bruised. He hadn't missed her intent. If she'd had more room to maneuver, he had no doubt she would have hit her mark already.

The stars above, how could she infuriate him and entice him at the same time. Her sweet scent filled him, made him want so much more. Even in this dire situation, he couldn't help wanting her. He'd waited for her for centuries and she was in his arms. Maybe not in the way he would prefer, but being cursed, he couldn't be fickle when an opportunity presented itself.

She stilled her movements and her breathing changed. For a breath of time, he didn't understand the meaning in her gaze until her tongue slipped out and licked her lips, moistening them. How could he resist such an invitation? He leaned down and kissed her, taking her under as he caressed those luscious lips into submission, but in the end, it was she who demanded obedience.

Minx, he thought, but his affection never wavered. She may not want to admit it yet, but she felt the connection, and he didn't refer to the bolt of electricity they sparked when they first touched outside. No, she responded to his touch. Her soul hungered for him as his did for her.

Now if he could just make her cooperate, he might be able to save his Callista before the beastie inside him took over and made its stand. Above all, it must protect the items it guarded. Already he could feel the gryphon threatening to take control, but he slammed down the urge to shift. The beastie would not ruin this precious moment.

Chapter Five

What was wrong with her? This guy wasn't even human. He could shift into a gryphon for God's sake. Calli's subconscious kept prattling on, trying to get her attention. Annoying! Right now, Darrien was every bit the man.

Her hands gripped Darrien's shirt and drew him closer, and his hand went to her waist. She could feel the warmth of his touch through her shirt, and his eyes... Those all so strange colored eyes gazed upon her as if he would give her the world, but right now she wanted one of his toe-curling kisses. She didn't have a long list of lovers, but none of them had ever kissed her like he had. His lips were like a caress her body craved, breathing life where she had remained dormant.

She almost believed he spoke the truth and she was indeed his soul mate. His mouth covered hers, and she closed her eyes, then on a sigh gave into the pleasure he offered. Her heart thumped so loud, she could hear the thumpity-thump in her ears, drowning out the world around her and, for a moment, she didn't fight it.

Her hand slid down the length of him as she contemplated her next move. He may have removed her weapons and tools, but perhaps he hadn't cleared out the nightstand drawer. There was one way to find out.

She nudged him toward the bed and inwardly sighed with regret at not being able to indulge in this fantasy they'd started. She had a hunch kissing wasn't all Darrien could do well.

Once they were backed up to the bed, she pushed him onto it and straddled him. She slid her hands over his arms, guiding them above his head, before leaning down to kiss him once more. A ploy meant to distract, and if his moan of pleasure was an indication, it was working. With one hand, she carefully slid open the drawer of the nightstand and reached inside. When her fingers touched cool metal, she almost smiled and probably would have if her lips hadn't been occupied. In the next second, she made her move. Her agile fingers manipulated the cool metal with a click to his right wrist and a click to the bedpost with the other half.

Darrien's eyes widened in alarm as he glanced at the cuffs then to her. But before he could grab her with his free hand, she leapt from the bed and out of reach. He yanked on the cuffs and to her relief they held fast.

"It's been fun, *Fly Guy*, but party time is over, and just so you know, I don't like playing second fiddle." He frowned at her analogy, and she shook her head. "You speak the language. Hell, you might even fit into society, but you think like an ancient being, don't you? In that regard, I could almost believe your claims you've been cursed for centuries, but let me put it to you simply. I'm not Callista, and I don't like to play dress up and pretend." She sauntered over to the table where Darrien had tossed her gear while she'd been unconscious.

"This isn't about me being a shifter then, am I right?" he asked, and there was a note of surprise in his voice. "That part does not trouble you. Yes?"

She glanced at him sprawled on the bed with his one arm cuffed and the other propping him up so he could peer at her. "My father used to tell me stories about beings that walked among the humans. Said he met a few."

"He did not fear these beings?" Darrien asked, and she could tell he was curious.

"No." she shrugged. "Everyone wants to be respected, right? They left my father alone, and he gave them the same courtesy."

"You say the words about respect, but these are your father's beliefs. What of you?"

"The world is full of different kinds of beings. So what? I never met any of the beings my father told me about, but it doesn't mean they weren't around. I have an open mind."

"I sense this about you," he told her.

She rolled her eyes. Of course he did. Right after he thought she was his soul mate, she said to herself, but aloud she voiced, "Anyway, the existence of shifters doesn't come as a complete shock to me. Heck, my cousin claimed he dated a werewolf, but up until tonight, I thought maybe he had a few screws loose, or at the very least was just making the story up for a few laughs. Go figure, he'd probably told me the truth."

He harrumphed. "You listened to your father's stories, but you didn't truly believe, did you?" He repositioned himself by scooting back to rest against the headboard, which sported slats, or he wouldn't be sitting like an offering for sinful delights. Pity she had to run.

She turned away because meeting his gaze just made all this so much more difficult. "Really, I'd like to sit down with you and have a deep discussion about shifters and other such beings, but I have to go." She didn't quite keep the terseness out of her voice. She couldn't let her guard down, and she had a feeling he was trying his best to distract her. She fastened her belt around her waist with quick jerky moves, indicating her frustration over this whole messed up situation. Her goal tonight: retrieve the stone. Done. Everything else was irrelevant.

"You cannot take the artifact." His voice broke through her reverie, and she paused. "It is dangerous," he said, not pleading or demanding. He simply spoke what he believed to be true.

Her gaze met his, curious over his calm approach. She thought he'd be breaking the headboard by now...or turning into the beast. Maybe there wasn't enough room for him to shift. "I've already taken it," she reminded him. "I just need to deliver it to the rightful owner."

His harsh laugh irked her.

"Do you have something to say?" she asked with her hand on her hip.

"I do not know who claims ownership of something only the gods should have, but if it falls into the wrong hands, it will be the end of mankind."

"Plu...eeese," she said, dragging out the word for effect. "Do you expect me to really consider your claims of doom?"

"Ponder this, Callista... Calli," he corrected, "you stole the stone from the Museum of Cursed Antiquities. Can you not deem the possibility that an unsavory sort wants the stone for their own personal evil deeds?"

"Okay, you piqued my interest. What can the stone do?" He hadn't explained exactly what it did. He'd only given her his doom and gloom speech.

"The one who possesses it will have the power to open the portal between life and death, and if the person performs the ritual on Halloween, it gives the conjurer more power to bring back many souls all at once."

"Because the veil is thinner this time of the year," she stated, familiar with the folklore surrounding Halloween. She'd been reading books about life after death, and not because her father had recently passed away. The subject had always fascinated her.

Professor Leander had told her she wanted the stone delivered to her before Halloween. She'd been adamant about the date. Had there been a more sinister reason behind it? She claimed if the stone was not returned by the morning of October 31st the institute funding the dig was going to close down the excavation site and call it a loss. They'd lose millions of dollars. That was the urgency to have the artifact delivered. The other… "Who in their right mind would want to raise the dead?" she asked.

"How well do you know this person who wants the stone?" he countered with a question of his own.

She really didn't know her client at all. She'd been hired, paid half the amount she requested, and she would be wired the remaining balance owed to her upon delivering it.

She hadn't taken an assignment since her father died. They'd been a team, retrieving items originally stolen from their rightful owners and who in returned paid a hefty finder's fee. The day her father died her thirst for adventure had suffered a blow. She hadn't only lost a father. She'd lost a friend, a confidant, and a business partner. Taking a job without him made her feel disloyal in some way, but her funds were dwindling, and the choice was made. She needed this job.

Professor Leander came from money, high society and all, and she'd shown Calli documents proving she was responsible for the stone at the dig site. Maybe it had been stolen, but it didn't mean the item wasn't as dangerous as Darrien claimed. "I'll tell you what," she told him, "I'll look deeper into all this, check out a few leads, and if what you say is true, I'll return the artifact to the museum."

His eyes were doing that weird glowing thing-y again. "You'll look into it?" His control seemed to be slipping. "This person who hired you will not allow you to look into it. If they know about the stone, they will stop at nothing to get it before the veil thins. You are in danger if you keep it. They will come after you."

"Oh, that's rich." She chuckled. "You mean she's worse than a gryphon? She's a respected professor, for God's sake."

"She is a professor?"

"Stop fishing for information," she snapped, more upset with herself than with him. She'd already revealed too much. She leaned down and ran her hand under the table, feeling for the duct tape. When her fingers grazed over it, she gave it a yank.

"What are you doing?" he asked.

"Never you mind," she told him as she pulled the gun free. She only kept a weapon on her for emergencies and this definitely qualified. To think she almost hadn't packed it for this assignment. The semi-auto was the Ruger LCP Revolver—lightweight, large enough to fit in her palm, but powerful enough to hold its own. This baby held five rounds. The perfect weapon for tight situations, just point and shoot.

She knew it was loaded, but she checked it anyway. Her gaze then found Darrien. His eyes were focused on her weapon and not her. "As you can see, I can take care of myself."

He shifted his gaze. "Are you going to shoot me?"

"Not if you don't come after me," she told him and unzipped the side pocket on her pants. She tucked the revolver inside and left it unzipped for easy access. "Now, I have to skedaddle. I have places to be, people to check out... So, ta-ta for now." She wiggled her fingers at him in a goodbye wave before heading for the door without even a backward glance.

"Calli, don't—" he still called after her.

She'd already stepped outside and closed the door behind her, muffling whatever request he was about to make. She really hated leaving him cuffed and vulnerable, but then he deserved to be left behind, didn't he? He did try to kill her after all – if she believed he could shift into a gryphon, and she was pretty sure he told the truth there. She'd only handcuffed him.

She pursed her lips as she recalled the events leading to this moment. The gryphon did come after her, but it hadn't harmed her, and the human side of Darrien hadn't harmed her either.

"No, don't go all soft now," she murmured. Her gaze landed on the bushes to the side of her, and she crouched down. Her hand brushed aside the dirt at the base of the plant, revealing the pouch she'd stashed at the last moment when she'd arrived at the motel. Her instincts had proven right on. She'd known the chase wasn't over when she left the museum. Hiding the stone was a must, so she'd faked dropping her keycard to hide it without being obvious. If Darrien had the stone in his possession, he would have been long gone by now.

She lifted the pouch and brushed off the dirt. She released the string and peeked inside. The stone was still there, nestled safely within its new confines. She gripped the pouch, but she didn't move toward her car. Why was she still hesitating about leaving Darrien cuffed to a bed?

'Cause you've questioned Professor Leander's motives for wanting the stone a million times before you committed to stealing it for her. 'Cause you always were suspicious of her, and Darrien reminded you of the fact.

She'd run a background check on Professor Leander—twice. She couldn't find any incriminating evidence. Not one thing to warn her not to take the job. Just the annoying niggling at the back of her mind, and now Darrien made her doubt her choices all over again.

Her hand wavered to her lips still tingling from Darrien's kiss. Good Lord, the man kissed as if he thirsted for her caress, and he wasn't selfish. He gave too. Boy, had he given. For a moment, she'd forgotten the reasons they were thrown together in the first place. "Too bad he longs for another woman," she murmured.

Another shriek of frustration resounded from the motel room, drawing her attention. She had a hunch Darrien wouldn't be kept prisoner for long. He may not be able to shift in the room, but his large biceps told her he wouldn't stay cuffed for long either. The headboard wasn't made of steel. He would break free eventually.

She hurried toward her vehicle. She'd check out

what Darrien claimed about the stone and go from there.

Chapter Six

Darrien shouted in frustration as he yanked on the handcuffs, but they held fast. He couldn't shift in such a small space without causing considerable damage to himself and the structure. He could ill afford either.

Wasn't he a halfwit? He should have been suspicious from the start when her actions proved amorous. He chortled in disgust at his own stupidity. Calli may be Callista reincarnated, but she in no way was the same woman he'd fallen in love with centuries before in Andros. Her soul had adjusted to this century and her upbringing had shaped her. Damn the stars above if he wasn't attracted to her anyway. He ran a hand over his face in frustration, inhaling deeply as he did so, then letting the air out of his lungs in a long-frustrated sigh. The little minx did not realize the danger she posed, not only from the person who hired her, but from him as well. His beastly side would sooner or later demand justice for her stealing the stone. He feared no matter his feelings for her, it would prove not enough, and the beastie would win.

He stared at the cuff surrounding his wrist and cursed again for being caught unaware. With his other hand, his fingers slid over the cool metal. "I am even a bigger fool," he grumbled, not because of the binds holding him fast, but because the handcuffs weren't anything special. They were not fashioned out of iron, but some other mundane metal of no consequence, nothing that would hamper his strength and abilities. He may not be able to shift into the gryphon because of the small quarters, but he could still shift into his elemental form. He let the elements slide over him and transform his body to ether.

Once free, he rematerialized into his human form and glanced at the clock on the nightstand. He had a few hours before he had to return to the museum or else find himself vulnerable as he turned to stone.

He threw open the door to the motel room, and immediately his gaze riveted to the car space where Calli had parked her vehicle.

Of course, he found it vacant. He'd expected no less, but still he cursed softly as he strode over to the spot. He inhaled deeply, finding her sweet scent beneath the car's more odorous aromas. He would be able to track her, and he shifted into the beastie, shielding his true self with magic.

Most humans could not perceive the Otherworldly realm, and still others dismissed it as a trick of the eye. There were only those few who could see through the trickery of magic and witness all things around them. Some went mad from it, others were leery and tended to stay clear of preternatural affairs, and still others were curious and worked beside such creatures who possessed more than a human side. Calli sensed the Otherworldly plane, even if she didn't wholeheartedly accept it as of yet.

The humans of the tribes that lived centuries ago lived among preternatural beings. It proved not a strange matter. As the ages forged on, humans began to fear preternatural beings with their abilities and their strengths. Perhaps they were justified. Not all preternatural beings cared for humans. Even in his clan, there had been those who despised the human tribes. They believed the humans used them for their purposes but didn't treat them with respect. Wars broke out, and despite the preternatural beings' strengths, the humans outnumbered them. The numbers of preternatural beings dwindled. Some became extinct. Others faded away into history until they became nothing more than legends and folklore, a preference the Otherworldly realm preferred.

Right now, he wanted to remain invisible and not give proof to his existence. He'd seen videos on the curator's computer. The hunt for the Loch Ness Monster and Big Foot were the biggest hits. Shifting to his beastie side was a personal moment he wished not to share with the world. The mortals lacking imagination would not understand and what they did not perceive as normal, they tended to hunt down and destroy. No, thank you, Zeus on high. He preferred the shadows.

Using his back paws to push off the ground and catapulting himself high enough for his wings to catch the wind, he soared even higher toward the heavens. His eyesight proved as keen as an eagle's, his wings as strong and sure as they supported his massive body high above the ground so he could search for Calli's vehicle. She drove a black sedan, what she perceived, no doubt, as inconspicuous.

While she'd been unconscious, he had rifled through the vehicle in hopes of finding the stone she secreted away. No sign of the stone, but he found her rental agreement for the vehicle, stating her name. It hadn't been the one she'd given him inside the motel room. So either she'd stolen the rental—he wouldn't put it past her—or she had many aliases with the credentials to back them up.

However, he remained sure she'd given him her true name inside the room. Perhaps she'd been a little disoriented and hadn't thought to give him something false, or she'd believed she could outsmart him and it wouldn't matter once the stone was in the hands of her client.

Wrong on both accounts. If he couldn't locate Calli in the next few hours, he'd search for her via the Internet. He'd pick up her trail again, even if it took a few nights to do so.

Damn the gods for limiting his abilities to the night. The artifacts were also in danger during the daylight hours. Having a human caretaker secure the building, while he waited out the endless hours in his deathlike state, didn't seem the wisest of choices, but there wasn't exactly a complaint box or a person he could chat with about the situation. The curse was all about remaining isolated. He was not worthy to be with anything other than objects that could not bleed…could not die…

For the last decade, a Mr. Andros guarded the cursed items, or so his stationary on the desk dictated. He wondered if the man was a distant relation to those who lived on his blessed Isle of Andros, but alas, there were no chummy meetings over tea. Once the sun had set, the man donned his hat, locked the building, and headed home—or so Darrien assumed. He really knew nothing of the curator's life, only what the man left scattered on the desk… his doodles and notes. He liked some sci-fi show and drew spaceships and such. They were interesting to say the least. His computer and the sites he visited were other such evidence. He tended to leave up sites like gardening, and articles about how to prepare chicken. Definitely, yawn worthy. The man had no taste, but his most annoying habit was his obsession for tea. Various teacups were left around the museum, some still filled to the brim. It was like the man would forget he'd brewed a blasted cup and then would prepare another.

Caring for the artifacts had always been done this way since ancient times. A curator ran the museum during the daylight hours, and then Darrien took over at night. Every few decades, the museum would be moved to a new location and a warding spell redone to keep the preternatural world at bay, less they be tempted to explore the cursed objects and use them for their own agenda. Humans couldn't be warded away, but the beast would take care of those who became too curious.

He assumed once the museum was moved to a different location, a new curator took over the daytime hours. Humans only lived so long.

The wind whipped around him, feathering along his body like a caress. He enjoyed his moment of freedom to fly above the world, even if it was to hunt for a wayward thief. He couldn't leave the building unless prompted to find a missing item, which had proven to be quite a while in between events. Come to think of it, he couldn't remember the last time he'd spread his wings in this fashion.

As much as he wanted to continue to fly, his senses kept gearing him toward the museum, which didn't seem to make a whole lot of sense when his thief was on the run. Perhaps the sun's attempt to peek over the horizon prompted his anxiety.

After a few more beats of his wings, he veered toward the museum, the apprehension growing stronger as he approached.

He landed with the grace of his kind before shifting into his human form. Then he sprinted to the front door only to skid to a halt as he rounded the corner.

"You!" he accused with confusion and surprise. His heart tripped then sped up as he swore softly. Calli stood in front of the museum with the pale light from the approaching dawn revealing her natural attributes. Her ginger-colored hair with strands of gold and dark auburn, rose-colored lips he had tasted yet longed for more, and a figure that sculptors would praise by carving statues in her honor.

She hadn't run after all.

Chapter Seven

"Hi, *Fly Guy*. Did you miss me?" Calli asked and her lips curved into a huge grin, loving that she'd surprised Darrien by showing up at the Museum. Heck, she'd been trying to go over her reasons for this bold move too.

After she abandoned him at the motel, she'd only gone so far before she realized she couldn't leave him. She needed answers about the artifact, and who better to ask than the person guarding it?

By the time she circled around, he'd already broken free of his confines...or rather somehow managed to slip out of the cuffs. She assumed he would take his gryphon form to search for her, but he probably wouldn't look for her at the museum. She headed there and hid her vehicle on the side of the building under the awning that appeared to be a private carport. She wanted the advantage of surprise.

Guess she got it if the "what-the-heck" look splattered across his face was any indication. "Thought we'd should have that little chat you spoke about," she said.

He glanced over his shoulder toward the horizon where the sky had turned shades lighter since her arrival. Sunrise couldn't be far off, and Darrien appeared apprehensive at the prospect, or maybe even fearful. That was silly, wasn't it?

She followed his gaze, but she could see nothing

out of the ordinary. The sky appeared clear with not a hint of an approaching storm. She tilted her head and peered at him standing there so strong and sure, and for a moment she imagined him in the Greek garb she'd seen him wear earlier this evening. He looked mighty fine in jeans and a T-shirt, but somehow the other clothing seemed more...him.

He must have sensed her staring at him, and he turned to meet her gaze. His eyes turned bronze then gold. She'd never seen such unusual eyes, but then she'd never met a shifter before tonight. Truly she should be frightened or at the very least uneasy around him, but her intuition told her he wouldn't harm her.

In his human form, he'd shocked her with his touch as if he held a live wire, but despite everything and despite he claimed the gryphon hunted down thieves, she didn't fear him.

For the moment, they weren't at battle for dominance and her gaze slid over him once more. This time she took her time, admiring his human form with curiosity. The man did have a nice physique, a cross between the ancient gods she'd seen depicted in paintings and a poster-boy for marine special-ops. Give him a nice military haircut and shave, and ooh-ah baby!

"You stare at me as if I am something you covet," he said. "And though I appreciate your admiration, it's not a wise expression if you do not want to follow through with it."

Her gaze riveted to his, and her eyebrows lifted as she realized his meaning. "Duly warned. So...do you want to let us in?" She nodded toward the door.

He did a little eyebrow raising himself. "Surely, I'm surprised you are not already making yourself at home. You had no difficulties earlier this evening letting yourself inside. And..." he pointed to the window void of glass. "It looks like locking up would prove ridiculous at this point, don't you agree?"

"Tsk tsk... Don't be rude."

"Rude? I am not the one being—" He shook his head, clearly exasperated, and murmured something in a language she didn't recognize, but she had a hunch by the tone it was not a litany of her finer qualities.

His hand reached for the doorknob, and it glowed a rich gold color as if it were recognizing a DNA imprint. A second later, Darrien pushed the door open, and he stepped aside to let her enter ahead of him.

"Who said a gryphon couldn't be polite?" she teased and threw him her sweetest smile as she strode inside. He didn't look overly pleased—probably because she couldn't quite say gryphon with a straight face. But then, he was inviting a thief into his house of treasures... Well, sort of treasures, if you were into cursed items.

Once the door was closed the room seeped into shadows, but she could make out the outline of Darrien and his eyes glowed in the dark with a gleam, reminding her he harbored the beast inside of him. "Do you have lights in this place?" she asked, expecting him to ignore her request, but without him moving—as far as she could tell—the lights overhead illuminated the room with a soft glow. "Nice trick." He lifted his shoulders in a shrug, making her wonder what other nifty tricks he could do. Shifting into a beast and back to human, flying, and slipping out of handcuffs came to mind.

"Why are you here, Calli?" he asked, forcing her to

focus on the reason she'd returned to the scene of the crime.

She did love the way his words slid off his tongue. He was Greek, she supposed. He was a gryphon, and she was sure the mythical creature's legends originated there. She almost chuckled. Mythical? Hmm…the myth was pretty much put to rest tonight. "I came back to the motel to free you," she said lamely.

"You did?" he asked with a frown as if he hadn't thought of the possibility.

"How else would I know you'd come back here? You somehow wiggled free." She paused and hoped he would fill her in on how he managed the magic trick, but he remained silent. "Well, okay then," she continued with her explanation. "I assumed you'd return to the museum eventually." Her lips curved into a grin. "I decided to go with my instincts. They've never steered me wrong yet."

"Is that so?" he muttered, not appearing in the least bit convinced.

Yeah, she hoped her freaky sixth sense hadn't gone whacky from her electrical jolt from earlier or otherwise this little detour may very well prove her last.

If she remembered her gryphon tales, they were like dragons. In the sense they probably snacked on thieves. She blinked back her thoughts of mayhem and possible death and focused. "I never trusted Professor Leander," she announced, catching Darrien's attention. At least he lost some of his hostile stance as he tilted his head in a birdlike fashion. She hurried on to explain. "Professor Leander is the woman who hired me. Not to say I trust you either, but maybe I should have all the facts before I decide what to do with the stone."

For a long moment, Darrien stared at her as if she were an object, he had yet to identify with his eagle-eye expertise, but then he spoke, "You are a strange thief, Calli Angelis."

"Are you trying to give me a compliment?"

"No," he said dryly and pursed his lips.

"Oh…well…" she cleared her throat. "Professor Leander wanted the stone and paid me well to retrieve it. She had documents and proof that the item belonged to her, or rather the Leander Corporation that funded the archeologist team and unearthed the site where the stone was found. I believed I was only retrieving the artifact and returning it to its rightful owner."

"She has lied to you," Darrien snarled, and his nostrils flared as if the thought of someone lying about owning the stone was a worse crime than her waltzing in here and stealing it.

"I kind of figured you'd say that," she said. "However, how do I know you aren't the liar in this scenario?"

"Gryphons never lie," he said with a huff of annoyance.

She tapped her forefinger on her chin and narrowed her eyes. "Now see, how would I know such a thing since I believed a gryphon to be a creature of mythology and not a beast coming to Noah two by two into the Ark."

Again his dark brow rose. "You do have a sense of humor, do you not, Miss Angelis?"

His sensual kissable lips slid into a smile making her knees weak. "How do you know it is Miss and not Mrs.?" she asked, just for the heck of it. Was it wishful thinking on his part?

"Because," his throaty, rough-worn voice said, "you're my soul mate, and I know you haven't been with another male in some time."

"Uh…what? Forget it." She held up her hands and took a step back. "Put on the brakes, buzz kill. Now you just ruined the moment, and I don't want to know how you figured out I haven't been with a guy in some time."

"Buzz kill?"

His frown only made him look more adorable, but his soul mate remark put a damper on flirting with him. She sighed with regret. The idea of sneaking another kiss just to see where it would lead had been tempting too. It's a good thing his words slapped her back to reality.

"Listen, I believe you're looking for this." She slipped her hand into her pocket and retrieved the pouch. "The stone's in here."

He moved so fast she would have sworn he had blinked into nothing then reappeared in front of her before she had time to blink herself. "What the—"

"Hand it over," he demanded, and she took another step back just for breathing space.

"I'm rather surprised you asked," she said. Her gaze landed on his eyes, the true tell of his emotions, and she swallowed the lump in her throat. "Can you stop with the weird-as-hell eye thing-y?"

His head tilted to the side, a movement reminding her of a bird of prey. "I do not know what you mean."

"Right. If you could only see what I'm seeing," she murmured more to herself than to him. "Anyway, before I give up the stone here, I want to know your story, and why I should give a flying crap what you say about it."

"You do know I could just take it from you," he said. The meaning behind his words did not go unnoticed, but at least he felt the need to clarify. "It wouldn't be pretty. The beastie inside of me demands justice. You stole what it guarded."

"But you won't hurt me, will you?" She smiled and took a chance her assumption was correct. "Because you believe I'm your soul mate," she added.

Chapter Eight

Calli stood perhaps five feet, four inches tall, petite, but what she lacked in height she certainly made up with her Amazon warrior tactics and bravery. She did not fear him in the least, and Darrien had no doubt the woman knew what the beastie was capable of doing. She hadn't run but came back to the museum to face him and demanded answers. She claimed he would not hurt her, but still she gambled with her life. "Perhaps you are correct, but you should not be so smug with your assumption. I would do all I could to keep my Callista safe, but I am also cursed." He waved his hand around the room in a full sweep to emphasize the many artifacts in the museum, and indicated he was also one of them. He watched her expression as her gaze took it all in.

There were chairs of various sizes and shapes; curio cabinets, some decorated with symbols, some with items on the shelves, some with none. Dolls with beautiful curls and pristine dresses stood at attention, while some were hideous with clothes that were blackened, as if someone had tried to burn them but hadn't succeeded. There were books stacked in one corner, and various clocks in sizes ranging from alarm clocks to Grandfather clocks in another. Of course, he knew she'd seen all of it when she broke in, but not when the overhead lights were turned on to highlight the objects with an eerie glow.

Finally, her gaze rested on him. "You are not an item," she told him and lifted her chin in defiance. "You're flesh and blood. You're real, and these are not." She pointed, but not at anything in particular.

He chuckled without mirth. "I am indeed an artifact as you shall soon learn for yourself. I am cursed and at the curator's mercy. I am neither alive nor dead, and I have traveled the world along with everything else in this museum, though I have never seen the sites of any of the places. My only purpose is to guard." Her brows furrowed and he didn't blame her for not realizing what he spoke of, but as soon as the sun rose high in the sky, he would once again be still as the objects around him, a soul trapped in the statue of a gryphon. "When you arrived tonight to steal Hecate's Stone, the official name if you didn't know—"

She rolled her eyes heavenward, and he had a hunch she'd known the name all along. Then he remembered the curators always labeled everything. She most likely noticed the card beside the artifact when her nimble fingers removed it from its berth. "You stumbled upon a statue of a gryphon, did you not?"

"How do you—" she began, but he interrupted her.

"Your hand caressed the statue as if you admired the fine art."

Her tongue slipped out to lick her lips as if they were suddenly parched. "The gryphon statue was you?" Her voice held a note of doubt.

"Cursed, remember?"

"Wow. The story just keeps getting better and better. I'm still getting used to the idea gryphons exist, and now you want me to believe you can turn to stone."

She chuckled, a nervous laugh as if all she learned was still being processed in her mind. She ran a hand through her hair. The long strands slid through her fingers, lifted away from her face, and floated down around her features again like flames of dark copper and even darker red. "Go on," she told him, and he had to blink to concentrate once more. His gaze caught sight of her striding over to a chair, intent on taking a seat.

"No, do not sit there!" he warned, panic making his heart beat faster and his body tensed as tight as the wire of a bowstring ready to spring forward. His booming voice made her jump, but at least it stopped her from making a big mistake. Her gaze swept over him, fully expecting an explanation, and he didn't disappoint. "It's the chair of a convicted murderer," he told her. " It was from his favorite restaurant where he had spent hours upon hours when he had been a free man. Upon the day of his execution, his last request was to have the chair you were about to place your derriere upon, delivered to his cell."

"So what. He cursed the chair?" she asked in confusion, and when he nodded, she threw up her hands. "Why would anyone do such a thing?"

"He didn't want anyone else to enjoy his spot in the restaurant. Of course no one believed the curse and the chair was returned to where it belonged, but when the patrons started succumbing to horrible deaths, everyone changed their minds soon enough."

Her lips pursed and she placed a hand on her slim hip, not appearing convinced in the least. "Come on. Everyone dies. I'm sure every death could easily be explained away."

"They died within a week of sitting in the chair,"

he added and her face paled. "Go on. Test the theory and plop down for a rest." He waved his hand at the item in question, knowing it would be a challenge she would not take. She was a thief, but she calculated her moves and didn't take unnecessary chances.

"Okay, fine," she finally said with a harrumph. "I believe you. So where do I sit?"

"At the curator's desk." He pointed to the wooden structure near the back of the room. "Should be safe enough. I haven't found the curator's body decaying among the artifacts."

"So nice to know," she said with a grumble as she strode over to the desk and pulled out the leather chair stationed behind it. She plopped into the chair and rolled it back so she could place her booted feet on top of the desk. All nice and comfy, she leveled her gaze on him. "Okay, spill it. Tell me the rest of your tale."

He shook his head with a sigh and glanced toward the broken window where the approaching day could be seen with the sky lightening with each passing second. "I do not have much time."

"You going somewhere?" she asked.

He turned to look at her. "Once the sun is high in the sky, I turn to stone."

Her haughty expression slipped from her face, and she swung her feet to the floor and scooted to the edge of the chair. "What do you mean? Like you're going to be a statue, and you can't just...I don't know," she snapped her fingers, "use your magic and be human again?" Then it must have all clicked into place. "You awaken when the sun sets," she said more to herself before her gaze riveted to him. "When I broke in, you were still sleeping, or whatever it is you do when you're frozen in time."

"Frozen in time is a good description, but when you arrived the awakening spell was at work. It doesn't just happen. It is a slow process."

She leaned on the desk and folded her hands. "Go on then. Tell me as much as you can before you can't."

"And what of Hecate's Stone you took?" He had to know she would not turn it over to the professor while he lay dormant and useless to stop the transaction.

"I'll keep it safe." He must have thrown her a skeptical expression because she added, "You have my word. I will not make a decision until I know all the facts about the stone and what it can do."

Still, he debated if he could trust her. Really, what choice did he have? He could let the beastie kill her here and now and be done with the charade, but his human half refused to let it harm her. Finally, he relented and gave her a nod. "I will have to trust you, I suppose."

"Jeez, thanks." She sat back in the chair once more. "Time's a ticking." She tapped her wristwatch.

At times, he believed her attitude was designed to irk him, but he let out a tired, exaggerated sigh and began his tale. "Gryphons were the guardians of treasures," he stated.

"I see nothing's changed," she interrupted before he could say more.

"Do you wish to hear the tale or not?"

She waved her hand in front of her. "Go on then."

"We were a noble tribe, both human and beast. We could shift at will, giving us an advantage some of the other shifters did not have."

"Was Callista a gryphon also?"

He shook his head. "She was not a gryphon, but a human. We grew up together, spent many afternoons talking and holding hands. She loved to talk, and she was clever and lovely…" He realized he was rambling and glanced at Calli. Her gaze was thoughtful, and he had feared she would think him a besotted fool.

"You loved her," she said as if she hadn't believed him when he had told her before.

"Yes, I loved her," he repeated in a low whisper. For a moment neither of them spoke, as if they were giving reverence to the love, he once shared with his sweet wife. "Callista's father approved our marriage for he loved his daughter more than any treasure he kept. He believed I would keep her safe always. He had no reason to doubt me since I had guarded his treasures well and had safeguarded his family from marauders for decades."

"But something happened," she said not as a question, but he nodded and answered her anyway.

"Yes. Isa…" He swallowed back the bile which threatened to choke him at the mention of the traitorous female who had stolen his love. "Isa was from my tribe and believed we should have been mated, but I did not love her the way she loved me. I cared for her, yes. I never encouraged her, but she mistook our friendship for more." He swallowed hard and fought the urge to cry out in anger and grief. When he had been free, and such emotions had plagued him, he would take to the sky for relief. Flying calmed his nerves, kept him centered. He glanced at the window with yearning.

The beast stirred inside of him, demanding to be released, but he couldn't indulge. The curse would not let him shift and use his gifts for comfort. He didn't understand how it knew the difference, but it did. He flew only to retrieve stolen artifacts. It was the only time his wings would obey him. He closed his eyes for a moment and took a deep breath. He hadn't expected the recounting of what happen centuries ago to hurt so much, but it was like a wound that wouldn't heal, and he was picking at it with his talons.

"Are you okay?" Calli asked.

He glanced at her and, in truth, worry marred her features. "It is difficult…" His voice broke, and he cleared his throat.

"It's never easy losing someone you've loved," she said. "No matter the how or the reasons why it happened."

Their eyes met, and for a moment he drew comfort and strength from her. He had to finish the story no matter how much it pained him to do so. "Callista and I were married for months, and we spent as many hours as we could together. We could not get enough of each other. It always amazed me how much I wanted to just be with her, look at her, or listen to her tell me about her day. She loved to fly. She'd sit upon my back with the wind blowing in her hair. She never feared being so high above the earth. Not when she was with me," he added, and his lips curved at the memory of her sitting upon his back and her laughter sweet and pure.

"She must have loved you dearly," Calli said, not as a question but as a statement.

He nodded. "Yes." He inhaled deeply and let his breath out again, preparing himself to tell the end to this story. "As Callista and I grew closer, Isa's jealousy took on a life of its own. I was foolish not to see it, but I was drunk on our love and believed everyone shared our happiness." His hand rubbed the back of his neck, his body already feeling the effects of the morning light. He felt stiff and achy and knew he had to hurry. "I would soon learn the ugly truth about Isa and how far she'd go to have what she wanted. Isa spun a fanciful tale and had me chasing a thief who did not exist. While I was on this merry chase, Isa cornered Callista at our home. My sweet wife never had a chance against a gryphon. Even in our human state, we are stronger than a mere person with no shifting abilities. Callista fought, that much was evident from the destruction left behind. Vases were broken and furniture was overturned..." He paused to take a breath and ran a hand through his hair.

"Normally, I'd say take your time," Calli said, "but the sun..." she nodded toward the window, and he turned to peer outside where the sky had lightened yet a few shades more.

He glanced at Calli again. "Isa ran a dagger through Callista's heart. When I arrived home, she no longer stood in the land of the living. Her life's blood had seeped out of her." He lifted his hands and stared at them. He had tried to stop the bleeding even when he knew it was too late. "There was so much blood."

"Did you go after Isa?" she asked quietly, but it drew his attention, and he lowered his hands.

"At first, I did not realize Isa was responsible for her death. Besides, I had something more pressing to face."

"Callista's parents?" Calli asked.

"Her mother wept uncontrollably, but Spiro her father was in a rage and wanted to have my head served on a platter. However, he thought of a more fitting punishment for me. A curse. Where I would never die but would never truly live either. I would be a guardsman of artifacts best forgotten for all time. Do you know how lonely forever can be?"

"I can't imagine."

For a long moment, neither of them spoke. It was a lot to digest. "What a horribly sad story," Calli voiced. "My heart breaks for all you've lost—your time with Callista and your chance for happiness, but…" She chewed on her lower lip as she worked out what she wanted to say. When she did, she leaned forward and rested her elbows on the desk. "In all the centuries, why haven't you found another woman to love? Please know," she hurried to say, "I'm not belittling your affections for Callista, but she could not be your one and only. Surely, there have been others." Her hand absentmindedly touched her lips, and he wondered if she were thinking of the kiss they'd shared.

He gave her a whisper of a smile. "I cannot leave this place, and even if I could, gryphons mate only once. We love truly and completely once we've found our soul mate. Callista was lost to me. She was a priceless treasure the world would never see again because I failed her. Don't pity me," he warned when she opened her mouth to speak, but he could see it in her eyes. She felt sorry for him, and he wouldn't have it. "I deserve this fate, but if there was some way to redeem myself, I would. On my very soul, I pledge that I would." He met her gaze and didn't waver as he let the true meaning of his words sink in.

The emotions flitted across her face—pity, anger, and grief being among them. Then her gaze leveled on him once more as the dawning of his words became clear. "You believe you can redeem yourself because of me. Because I look like her, right?"

He had hoped as much, but not just to redeem himself. He loved Callista. To have her back with him again…even for a moment… He sighed heavily. "You are Callista." Calli opened her mouth to probably deny the fact, but he held up his hand to silence her. "Please, hear me out before you say more."

She nodded and settled in her seat once more.

"My very soul feels her in you, but you are also different. Perhaps each rebirth also allows for the soul to have its own individuality."

She leaned back, a frown marring her features. "You'll have to forgive me if I don't buy into the whole reincarnation bit."

"Did you believe gryphons existed before tonight?" He lifted a brow, daring her to answer with the truth.

"Well… no." She brushed a wayward strand of hair behind her ear. A gesture Callista did often when she was deep in thought, or if something perplexed her and she needed to work it out. "I may not be an expert on Greek mythology," she said, "but I don't remember reading very many stories about gryphons, and your love story and Callista's seems like a tale that would have made the books."

"Spiro, Callista's father," he clarified, "made sure the gryphons were forgotten, or so he hoped, to achieve further punishment. To be forgotten is the worse curse of all, don't you agree? It's as if you never existed, but somehow the word gryphon has slipped into the languages all the same, however our glorious tales are all but gone." He shook his head as he remembered his tribe, his mother, father, sister, and all the others. As far as he knew, he may very well be the last of his kind.

"I'll remember you," Calli said and drew his attention.

Before he could comment, before he could tell her how much those words meant to him, the curse took hold, and he froze. The sun was in full power, and he no longer could be. He felt the shift upon him and the hardening of the blood in his veins...his limbs. He would be a statue once more.

Chapter Nine

"What's happening?" Calli flew to her feet as she witnessed Darrien's body contorting at an alarming rate. His skin paled to a ghastly shade of white-gray then a horrible gurgling sound escaped his lips as if his breath had solidified in his throat. The awful truth dawned on her of what was happening. "The curse," she said in both awe and apprehension. "Oh, Darrien." She felt the tears prick her eyes at seeing him so vulnerable, and the agony he went through as the curse took hold and contorted his body into the statue he would soon become.

He told her this is what would happen, but something else was taking place too. Her hand slipped into her pocket to retrieve her cell phone. Recording this seemed somehow important and she didn't hesitate, sliding her thumb over the record button. But as Darrien's change progressed, she felt guilty to be witnessing such a private event.

"Omigod," she mouthed, but she couldn't seem to tear her eyes away. Frustration and curiosity did a strange dance inside of her as she watched transfixed as the process took place. She couldn't look away.

Just when she thought nothing more horrific could happen, Darrien's body divided as if he were two completely separate beings—a man and a gryphon. It was like his soul was being torn in two. The gryphon struggled, its wings fluttering to life, large and beautiful like an eagle's majestic span, but on a much bigger scale. It bellowed and its eyes—Darrien's eyes met hers. Her hand flew to her mouth to stifle a cry, and she had to force herself not to go to him. She could do nothing to help him, but she could stay so he knew he wasn't alone.

Her gaze then centered on the human essence which separated as soon as the gryphon side of Darrien's existence completely hardened into the statue. This human form was not solid, but like a ghost, transparent. It didn't seem to notice her at all as it strode or rather floated toward the front door as if to leave the premises. She stared wide-eyed for two full seconds before she went after him, still filming as she wondered where he was heading.

He floated through the front door, and she immediately threw it open to give chase. She halted on the landing then caught sight of him heading around the corner, and she hurried after it, only to slide to a stop when she spotted the ghostlike figure standing by a vehicle parked in the carport next to her car. She'd noticed the vehicle earlier but didn't question it since it was dusty and had obviously been sitting there for a long time.

Then the most amazing thing happened, Darrien solidified into a human form, clothes modernizing into slacks, dress shirt, tie, and cardigan. Black-rimmed glasses materialized on the bridge of his nose, making him appear studious and perhaps a bit geeky, but with a rough edge.

For a long moment, he just stood there by the car, staring at it. His eyes seemed to shift back and forth like when a person dreams, only his eyes remained open as the process took place.

"Darrien?" she called to him and lowered her phone.

He jumped at the sound of her voice and stumbled back as he spoke, "Oh dear, you gave me such a fright." His voice sounded different. Still a deep masculine baritone, but the way the words flew off his tongue... Then it dawned on her. There had been no sign of an accent, which revealed his Greek heritage. Instead, this version of Darrien sounded British, if she could go by his over exaggerated dialect that would make a true Brit cringe. Interesting development. She wondered what else would prove different about him.

"I didn't mean to startle you," she told him and smiled, hoping to put him at ease. She wasn't sure what Darrien remembered about his change inside, but since he never mentioned any of this, he probably didn't remember a darn thing. He seemed to be a very thorough man, a warrior who'd once been in charge, but this part of his essence appeared a bit frazzled.

Darrien's frown deepened, but she couldn't be sure if it was because she stood there or that he was still disoriented from his ordeal. She cleared her throat and tried for small talk. "I'm interested in viewing the museum," she told him. "I've heard you have some interesting objects on display. I'm writing a thesis and my topic is about if items can be cursed."

Nerdy Darrien, as she decided to refer to this version of Darrien, pushed his glasses back on the bridge of his nose as he assessed her, not with interest as a man who was attracted to her, but with suspicion. He definitely was not the same man she'd spoken to inside the museum ten minutes ago. This version didn't know her or trust her, but she had to somehow change his mind.

"How did you hear about the museum, Miss…?" he asked.

"I'm Calli Angelis." She stepped closer with slow easy steps as if she was dealing with a frightened animal, and Nerdy Darrien was doing a great imitation of one. She didn't want him bolting before they had a chance to chat.

His gaze slid over her, and his dark brows furrowed again as he blinked a few times in a row. For a moment, she thought he might remember her, but then his features smoothed as if those memories weren't allowed to surface. "Miss Angelis—"

"Calli," she corrected as she took another step closer and offered her hand.

He stared at her outstretched palm for a second before gripping her hand, but the electrical shock made them both pull back in surprise. She'd experienced the same thing when his other half had grabbed her hand— flesh-to-flesh contact, she realized—though, that encounter had been more explosive. "Sorry about that," she said as she rubbed her palm.

Darrien waved it off. "Static electricity. It happens. Forgive me, but why are you here again? We don't have many visitors. This is more of a storage facility than anything else." He still seemed wary of her, and she wasn't sure how to put him at ease.

"Do you really believe the items you guard…I mean, oversee are cursed?" she asked.

"Oh, indeed I do, Miss…um…Angelis." His tone was haughty, as he peered at her over the rim of those adorable glasses. "If you think this is a game," he continued without a beat, "you can just run along home now." He actually waved her away like he would shoo away a pesky fly.

Her brows rose, and she almost smiled at how serious he seemed, but she could ill-afford to piss off this version of Darrien. She didn't have much time before she had to contact Miss Leander and hand over the stone. She really didn't fancy the idea of sharing the world with the living dead. She'd seen enough zombie movies to know it didn't end well for the living.

"No, I don't think this is a game. I take curses seriously. You see, I am in possession of a cursed item, and I would like to discuss what I should do with it. You come very highly recommended. Please, don't send me away." She turned on her charm, or at least hoped she did, and smiled sweetly with a slight bat of her eyelids. "Please, I need your help. I don't know who else I can ask." She kept her smile in place and hoped she hadn't poured it on too thick in the damsel in distress department. She really didn't play that role very well.

Nerdy Darrien pulled on his tie as if it had suddenly constricted his airway. "Fine. Why don't I put on a pot of tea, and we'll have a nice chat? Yeah?"

She did love this version of Darrien as much or even more than the *beastie-I-am-cursed* version. There was just something endearing about him, she thought as she followed him around to the front of the museum.

As they made their stroll, her mind skipped ahead to a story she would spin for his benefit. Obviously, thinking and walking proved too much for her. She never noticed Darrien ceased to take one step in front of the other and plowed right into him. All plots vanished from her mind, she stumbled and almost ended up on her rump, but she had great reflexes and her hand snaked out, grabbing Darrien's cardigan to steady her. He glanced over his shoulder with concern. "Sorry," he apologized.

She let her hands fall to her side, but before she could question him about his great imitation of a tree suddenly taking root, he strode away from her to plant himself in front of the busted window. She'd forgotten about that little mishap last night.

"I can't believe this," he stated, probably not to her, but just blowing off steam. "Bloody vandals." Then his anger turned to concern. "Oh, I do hope they didn't take anything. This is an utter disaster." He hurried past her, producing a key he had stuffed in the pocket of his cardigan. Obviously, this version of Darrien didn't have nifty gifts like opening locks with his palms. He needed a key like the rest of the mere mortals.

Darrien halted when he spotted the door stood slightly ajar. He cursed softly as he nudged the door open the rest of the way.

With a sigh, she followed him inside and came to stand next to him as he stared at the window, or rather lack of one. His brows knitted together, and she was beginning to think this was an expression he wore often. "How very odd," he commented, and it made her stare at the window frame too.

"What is?" she asked.

He glanced at her. "It appears as if the glass was broken from the inside. See how there are very little fragments on the floor?" He strode closer to the windowsill and peered out. "The shards litter the ground outside."

"Uh…yep, very odd," was all she could muster to say.

"I'm sorry, Miss," he turned to face her, "but we'll have to postpone this meeting. I'll have to call someone out to repair the glass and do an extensive inventory to make sure nothing was stolen. It will take me all day, if not longer, to do a proper job of it." He started past her, but she placed a hand on his arm, and he halted his steps to gaze at her expectantly.

"I can't leave just yet. I think once you hear me out, you'll understand why."

His gaze shifted to where her hand rested on his arm.

"Darrien? Did you hear me?"

He met her eyes. "You were saying?" Then he frowned. "How do you know my first name? I never told you."

Now he notices. She only addressed him as Darrien outside in the carport, but then maybe he still had been a tad loopy from his transformation. "We have a mutual… friend," she settled on for lack of a better description of their relationship. Reincarnated lovers didn't seem a good place to start.

"A mutual friend?" he asked. He had an absent-minded professor look about him. She would bet this version of Darrien misplaced things on a regular basis. Must be a side effect of the curse and the whole soul-splitting ordeal…or whatever the process was called.

"Earth to Darrien," she said to gain his attention.

His eyes came into focus, the golden brown a darker shade. "Sorry, just thinking," he told her. "I can't deny it. You do have me curious, Miss…"

"Calli, will be fine."

"Miss Calli."

"Uh… oh, never mind."

"Good then. If you don't mind me making a few calls…"

"Not at all. Please take your time. I'm not in a hurry."

"Come along then," he said as he turned away and headed toward the back of the museum. "Nothing will be open yet anyway. I'll ring a place at a more respectable hour and make the arrangements to have the window fixed. Until then, we might as well have a proper cup of tea as I promised you." He strode by his desk where the statue of the gryphon sat strong and true.

He'd only taken a few more steps, before he came up short and whirled around to stare at the beast, who in return seemed to be staring back. She had to admit it was a little disconcerting.

Darrien lowered his glasses to the tip of his nose as if somehow his eyewear had become faulty. "What in the bloody hell is going on here?"

"Is something the matter?" she asked, all innocent and smiles, but knowing perfectly well he was referring to the statue and wondering how it had moved from the back room to here.

He whirled toward her as if a response danced on the tip of his tongue, but then he must have decided to rein in his explanation for his sudden outburst. Most likely knowing any claim he issued would sound like he'd lost his mind. Instead, he shook his head as he pushed the glasses back on the bridge of his nose. "Nothing." He turned and continued, reaching the swinging door situated behind the desk. His hand pushed it open to reveal a kitchen hidden behind it. The museum did have all sorts of perks, but she supposed it would have to since a cursed being was trapped inside.

Callista's father had been a real piece of work. He cursed Darrien for something that wasn't his fault, a curse which trapped him forever within a stone statue and in a man who surely felt the loss of his other half but hid behind his work to compensate for it. Nerdy Darrien and Beastie Darrien could never truly live.

"How do you take your tea?" Seconds ticked by before she realized he'd spoken to her. "Tea?" he repeated when she met his gaze. "How do you take it?" he clarified.

She had no idea since she really was a coffee kind of gal. "Uh…I'll take it however you do."

He gave her a slight nod, seemingly satisfied with her response. Once they had their teacups in hand, they headed out of the kitchen. He offered her a seat in the chair, but she decided on the desktop, feeling he may need to sit comfortably when she gave him a recap of her evening with him…or rather his other half.

He finally took a seat too but took forever to find a comfortable position. He repositioned himself so many times she was about to ask him if he needed to go to the restroom, but she realized it was her close proximity making him squirm in his seat. She would have chosen another chair, but she wasn't going to take a chance of sitting in one of the cursed ones and have the enchantment transferred to her. No sir-ee Bob, and thank you very much.

She sipped the brew and was pleasantly surprised. She liked the taste of black tea with a splash of milk. Go figure.

Finally, Darrien settled, and he raised his teacup that appeared way too dainty in his large hands. Yet, she had to admit, he handled it with finesse and didn't look a bit like a sissy when he pressed it to his lips. He indulged in a respectful taste of his brew before lowering the cup and meeting her gaze. "You were going to tell me about the cursed item of yours," he said. He was all business—like now that he'd had his morning fix. "Please proceed if you will," he encouraged further.

He wasn't going to like what she had to tell him anymore than she liked telling it. "I'm going to give it to you straight because... Well, we just don't have the time."

"We?" he asked, catching she'd included him in this scenario.

"Sit back, Fly Boy. Storytelling isn't my thing, so bear with me and know I do apologize for my lack of finesse."

Chapter Ten

Darrien listened to Calli's story with minimal interruptions, but truthfully hadn't known what to say. Dear God, the story the woman spun, and she didn't believe herself a storyteller—curses and mythical beasts. Surely, this story should be on the bestseller list for fantasy reads, or at the very least, a hopeful for the next Sci-fi show on the telly.

"...and then we came in here," she finished with a long sigh. She sipped her tea and obviously waited for his response, but he could only manage to stare at her in disbelief.

He forced himself to close his mouth before she thought he had a stroke. He still may have one. This woman—this thief, so she coined herself—claimed he was a cursed man, not any cursed man, but a gryphon as well. Hence the reason for the unorthodox nickname of *Fly Boy,* she'd called him earlier, he could only surmise. His gaze shifted to the beastie sitting there regarding him with attitude. He blinked, hard and ran a hand through his hair, not caring it would probably stand up on end. This had to be a bloody joke, one he'd not been made privy to the reasoning behind it.

He stared at Calli with her long ginger-colored hair, big moss-colored eyes and... His gaze traveled down the rest of her, taking in every womanly attribute. The woman truly tried his restraint—not that he'd be in her league or that she'd look at him at all if she hadn't been deranged. Yes, that was possibly the case here. This woman was mad as a box of frogs, and he needed to ring the police before she came unhinged. Truly, he didn't know what she was capable of doing, but he had a hunch she'd do it well.

He caught sight of the broken window. Perhaps she'd smashed it with the intention of playing this elaborate jest. His gaze shifted to the gryphon again. The beast stared at him with those unnerving golden-bronze eyes. The darn thing put him on edge, always had.

Finally, he leveled his gaze on Calli once more. She did lay claim to being a thief, but she couldn't have moved the heavy statue by herself, could she?

She could have an accomplice, he thought. And didn't that just up his panic response. No, the woman was alone or else the other guy...or gal would have joined them by now.

He smiled at the would-be-thief, knowing he'd have to tread lightly and play nice with the pretty nutter, at least until he could ring for help, but at this precise moment he needed to answer her. "It's a lot to take in. Yeah?" he said and leaned back in his chair. He folded his hands, pressing the tips of his forefingers together and tapped his chin. He glanced at the phone on his desk and ruled out using it, since she would subdue him before he could dial a number. Not that the itty-bitty thing could take him down. He wasn't completely useless, but who knew if she carried a weapon.

"Tell me about it," she said as she eyed him over the rim of her teacup then indulged again. She really had no idea how to drink tea properly. One simply did not gulp it down like a pint of beer.

"I'll have another," she announced as uncouth as a barmaid, which just proved his point.

He stared at the cup for a second before he reached for it with a sense of triumph. This was his opportunity. There was a phone hanging on the wall in the kitchen. "I'll be right back." He stood, but she did also. He couldn't have her traipsing along with him. His gaze caught site of the large leather-bound book sitting next to the computer. "Um… I can manage fine. While I'm warming the water in the kettle, you can browse through this." He placed the cup down to reach for the book.

"What is it?" she asked, curiosity lighting her eyes.

"It's a catalog of the cursed items here in the museum. I'm sure you'll find Hecate's Stone you speak of listed with the history of how it became cursed." He pushed the book toward her.

"Thanks," she said and plopped down in his seat, making herself right at home. He picked up the cup again and wondered if he should have been so willing to give her the information, but it proved too late to second-guess his willingness to help her now. He hurried toward the kitchen. At the door, he chanced a glance to see if her curiosity was still piqued. She flipped through a few pages then paused as if to read one of the passages. He let out a sigh of relief he'd been holding and turned away.

Once in the kitchen, he placed the teacup on the stove and rushed to the phone, mounted on the far wall. He'd only picked up the receiver and punched in two numbers when he heard the kitchen door behind him open. He closed his eyes and cursed.

"Hang up the phone, Darrien," she told him, her voice cold and unnerving.

He turned to face her and noticed the revolver. It fit nice and snug in the palm of her hand, but it might as well have been a machine gun for all it mattered. His hands flew above his head in surrender. "I'm sorry, but I had to try."

She rolled her eyes heavenward before she leveled her gaze on him once more. "I suppose you did have to try. I would have if I were in your shoes. I did warn you, I'm not a great storyteller, but I thought you and I had an understanding. We can't call the cops, assuming that's who you were about to call."

He didn't bother denying the fact. "What now? Are you going to shoot me?" he asked.

She waved the gun at the other room. "I want to show you something."

He lifted a brow but didn't argue. The woman held a gun on him, so options were at a minimum.

"Sit," she demanded once they were back at his desk. He did and chanced a look at her. She surprised him by placing the gun down on the desktop. "I don't want to hurt you, Darrien," she told him, and he wished she wouldn't use his first name with her easy-on-the-ears voice. It distracted him, and he needed to stay focused if he wanted to get out of this alive. "Believe me, I don't," she added for good measure. She must have sensed he didn't believe her.

"But you will if I don't cooperate," he said.

"No." She actually seemed insulted that he would suggest such a notion. "I need your help." She let out a frustrated sigh. "I really wish you weren't the one here right now. I need him." She pointed to the gryphon.

"The statue talks to you?"

"Yes. I mean no." She moved so fast to sit down on the desktop, it startled him. He pushed back in his chair with his feet, the wheels sliding him along until her boot caught the edge of the chair, and she rolled him back in front of her. She did all this without pausing as she prattled on about her conversation with the gryphon, or rather his other self. If he were inclined to believe such a preposterous story.

"You can shift to your human side also when you're united with your gryphon self, you see?"

No, he didn't see. "Let's for a moment believe what you've told me is all true, and you are indeed the sane one here."

She opened her mouth to no doubt complain, but he held up his hand to halt her words.

"Let me finish, if you will. How do you propose I help you when…he," he waved toward the statue and all its finery, "could not?"

"You keep forgetting. You are the gryphon."

"Right-o."

"You said the items in the museum are all cataloged. Find the gryphon in that book of yours. You weren't lying about the contents, were you?"

No, he hadn't lied, but she didn't wait for his response. She pushed the book toward him and waited for him to comply with her request.

He had a hunch if he just dismissed her and insisted she leave the premises, he'd have a real fight on his hands. The gun lay as a reminder giving him no other choice. She claimed she wouldn't hurt him, but really, did he want to take the chance? He'd have to play along for now.

With a sigh, he leaned forward in his seat and scanned the contents, looking for the entry regarding the gryphon. A few minutes later, he came across it in living color. There was a sketch of the beast, not a photo. The item obviously had been with the collection for a long time. He read the description of the curse handwritten beneath it. "Cursed to guard treasures," he read out loud. "Never one with itself," he said with less confidence. What did that mean? Not one with himself. "Darkness is for the beast as light is for the human soul." He stared at the passage. Calli might have told him a similar story, but it didn't mean it actually referred to him. He was about to tell her so, but then she shoved her mobile phone in front of him. A video played, and it took him a second longer to register what he viewed.

He shook his head in disbelief, but how could he deny what she'd caught on film? He bloody well shifted into the gryphon then something resembling a ghostlike being… "This cannot be real," he said, but his gut told him what he viewed was indeed all too real. He played it again. Then again…and yet again. All the blood seemed to rush to his head and the room tilted. "I don't feel so…well," he said. A silvery light blurred his vision right before everything went black.

Chapter Eleven

"Darrien!" Calli cried as she jumped off the desk and tried to stop him from toppling from the chair. He may be Nerdy Darrien, but it didn't make him any less impressive in size. She only managed to fall over too, with him landing on top of her. All the air went out of her in a whoosh.

"Darrien…ouch…uh…" she grunted and shoved at his shoulders. Just her luck, his geeky side was a fainter. She shoved again, trying to squirm free. "God, you are heavy. Ugh! Move, will you?"

He groaned in protest, but she wasn't entirely sure it had anything to do with his unconscious state, but rather about her rubbing against him as she tried to wiggle free. "This cannot be happening," she murmured, but apparently it was. He didn't roll away as she hoped. Instead, she only managed to ignite his passion. His lips found hers and he kissed her…again. Or rather, Nerdy Darrien kissed her. It seemed the curse could not control some things. His ability to kiss proved one of those things. Boy, did Beastie Darrien and Nerdy Darrien have this in common.

Passion overrode her need to be free, and her eyes fluttered closed as she took what he offered, savoring all the subtle variations of his kisses. Her fingers spread into the silky softness of his hair. A moan of pleasure escaped her lips. The sound surprised her so much, a glass of cold water in the face couldn't have done better. Her eyes popped open as reality came hurdling back. What she was doing proved to be all kinds of wrong. He wasn't really conscious, even if his libido had awakened to greet her. She moved her head to the side, breaking their lip-lock and taking a well-needed breath. Then she promptly slapped his face. "Wake up!"

Darrien sputtered and his eyelids snapped open. He blinked a few times in rapid succession as if he had trouble focusing without his glasses.

"Calli?" he asked, his voice shaky and disoriented. Then he must have noticed the intimate situation they found themselves in. His face turned three shades of red as he scrambled off her. "Sorry," he said as he searched for his glasses, his hands outstretched and his fingers gingerly feeling the floor.

Yep, he did a great imitation of being a blind man, only it seemed he wasn't acting. He was truly sight impaired.

She spotted the eyewear and reached for them. "Here," she said and knelt in front of him to place the glasses on the bridge of his nose. Their eyes met and for a moment she thought perhaps he would kiss her yet again. Her heart fluttered in response, and her breath caught in her throat just thinking about those lips on hers. She really didn't understand this immediate attraction. Love at first sight was not her MO, and lust at first sight wasn't either.

If he loves me—she was not going there. Kissing didn't mean love. "It's a good start," her mind casually mocked her. "Stop it."

Darrien frowned at her outburst and lifted his hands to the side. "I'm not doing anything."

She waved him away. "I know. Put your hands

down," she ordered, which didn't put him at ease. "Sorry. I'm just... Forget it, will you?" She glanced away. She couldn't stare into those hypnotic eyes of his and stay focused on what mattered here.

Starting a relationship with any guy was too much to handle in her line of business. Relationships were about trust, and she'd have to lie about where she went and the jobs she pulled. Some people were too narrow-minded to appreciate her line of work. As for Darrien? Heck, he had his own issues. Split souls proved a new one on her, but the confusion would be more than she wanted to take on. It would seem like she was cheating on Beastie Darrien if she were to kiss Nerdy Darrien...and vice-versa. No, she couldn't. No, kissing either of them, even if both Darriens could make her toes curl.

"I am sorry," Darrien said again, and he did look contrite. His face remained flushed and his eyes bright. "I don't understand what came over me," he added and pursed his lips.

Her cheeks felt hot too. "Don't worry about it. Can't fault you for something you didn't know you were doing. Besides it wasn't all that bad." His gaze riveted to hers and she wished she hadn't added that last part.

He cleared his throat. "Well then," he said and rose to his feet, offering her a hand up.

"Thank you." His grip proved strong and warm and made her wish he would pull her into his arms. "Uh...we should...uh..." Her thoughts not only tripped her into stuttering, but it also startled her enough that she stumbled right into his hard chest to receive her wish. Darrien's arms went around her, bracing her fall and bringing her up close and personal all over again.

"I have you," he told her.

The funny thing was, she believed he did, in more ways than one. She steadied herself and gripped his forearms as she took a step away, if only to take a well-needed breath and gain control of her emotions. "Aren't we the stumbling duo?" She chuckled as she brushed a strand of hair behind her ear. Darrien froze and stared at her as if the gesture was out of the ordinary.

"What?" she asked. "You aren't going to faint again, are you?"

His eyes focused then, and he blinked. "Faint? No, of course not, but I had the strangest feeling of déjà vu. Quite put the hairs on my arms on end." He rolled back his sleeve to show her the evidence. "The way you tucked your hair behind your ear... Well, it seemed familiar."

"Oh..." She couldn't quite keep the disappointment out of her voice. She thought he'd referred to their kiss. Guess she needed some work on her technique to make it memorable. Her fingers itched to tuck another wayward strand behind her ear, but she held herself in check. "Like I told you, we've already met. You're probably picking up on last night's introductions."

"Yeah. Right-o. So you've said. Perhaps you're correct." He glanced at the book opened to the page dedicated to the gryphon. Then his gaze shifted to the real deal, the statue in the flesh. Well, in stone anyway. "I'm a gryphon," he said more to himself than to her, as if he wanted to try out the statement and see how he felt about it. He chuckled, but she knew he was not happy he'd been forced to learn such a secret. "A gryphon is a fearless beast," he said. Sadness dimmed his eyes to a dull gold brown. "I am no such thing, I'm afraid."

"Noble and loyal are traits also, and I bet those adjectives fit you."

"You know nothing about me, Miss Angelis."

She gave him a smile. "I believe we established I know more about you than you do." Her statement didn't exactly cheer him. "Listen, we'll sort this all out later. Right now I need your help discovering who Professor Leander truly is and why she's so determined to have Hecate's Stone."

"Perhaps we should focus on how she knew about the stone in the first place?" he countered, and his left brow rose. "I can assure you she never owned the object in question. Even if her corporation funded the dig, they would not deliver it into her hands. There are certain channels one would follow to ensure the safety of the artifact. The fact that she hired you without the press and she wired your money to an offshore account only proves she is hiding something."

"She convinced me otherwise with her story about the company losing their funding. She claimed if the press got wind that an artifact went missing, it would appear as if they were incapable of guarding the site against fortune hunters. They would be shut down." She pointed to the computer on his desk. "Does that work?"

"Of course." He took the steps separating him from the desk and sat down in the chair. He reached for the button on the lower left corner of the monitor and the screen lit up. "What do you want to look up first?"

"I tried to research Professor Leander, but I only came up with things about her charitable contributions and her papers on Grecian history and art. Every article praised her expertise on the subjects, but I have a hunch this was a front for what she truly does with her free time. Let's see if we can dig a little deeper and find out what it is before I have to meet with her." She glanced at her watch. "At the very least, I'll need to phone her with an update."

"No matter what we find out, she cannot have the stone," Darrien reminded her. "It's dangerous and no one should be able to wield such power."

She'd already decided she wouldn't turn it over, but she wanted answers. She didn't like being used, and especially when it involved her being responsible for a possible zombie apocalypse. "She's not getting her hands on it," she said aloud, "but I have a hunch we're dealing with someone who can make our lives miserable if she doesn't get her way. She didn't strike me as the bow down and go away type."

"If Professor Leander is as powerful as you claim, why didn't she just waltz in here and take the stone herself?" His brows furrowed as he thought about the question he voiced. Then his eyes lit up like he'd been given the best gift ever. "She's a preternatural being. The museum is warded against Otherworldly beings from willy-nilly taking items as they please. Why else would Professor Leander not take action herself?"

She really did like the way he talked. *Willy-nilly.* Cute. She cleared her throat and tried to focus on the dilemma at hand and not how adorable Nerdy Darrien appeared sitting behind the desk, all straight-laced and proper. She wasn't doing a very good job of being professional. All she could think about was removing his glasses and running her hands through his hair while she kissed him. If she pushed his chair back, his lap would be available for her to sit on and try out the fantasy.

Stop it, she silently scolded herself and bit the inside of her cheek to put a halt to her daydreaming. This is what happened when she didn't get enough sleep. She became *willy-nilly* silly. She chuckled and covered her mouth.

"Did I say something to amuse you?" Darrien asked and gave her a stiff upper lip.

"No, I'm sorry. I'm slaphappy here. I could use a cup of coffee. Do you happen to have some stashed in the kitchen?"

"Sure thing. I have a notion to have a cup now and again." He pushed back the chair and stood.

As she followed him into the kitchen, she tried to remember what they were talking about. Oh, yeah… "You mentioned the museum is warded against preternatural beings," she commented. "How do you know this?" She had assumed he didn't know about the preternatural world, but then again, he was the curator for cursed artifacts. How could he not know?

Darrien opened a pantry next to the refrigerator, stocked with cans, flour, cereal, and all kinds of other goodies. "If you look closely at the museum walls," he said, "you'll notice there are fine lines, symbols, and drawings. Those are the wards preventing supernatural creatures from entering."

Her brow furrowed, not because of his explanation about wards and etches on the wall, but because she wondered who stocked his pantry. Beastie Darrien certainly couldn't, and Nerdy Darrien materialized every morning for the daytime job. She pushed away from the wall and strode over to take a closer look. She even went as far as picking up a can of beans. "Feels real."

"Why wouldn't it?" Darrien asked and stared at her in confusion. He then glanced at the coffee can he held.

"Who does your grocery shopping?" she asked.

"I do," Darrien said. "Once a month I drive into town and pick up a few items."

"So you can leave the museum for long periods of time."

He lifted a shoulder. "I suppose, but I don't leave often, and I never had the need to do so."

"You never craved companionship? Never wanted to just close up the museum and never return? What about vacations?" She wanted to know everything about this version of Darrien. Maybe if she put it all together, she could somehow help. Who knows, maybe even put an end to his curse.

"I tried…numerous times, but I always…" His gaze met hers. "Bollocks. I would get an anxiety attack and decide against it. Even the jaunts to the market put me on edge if I dallied too long." He sighed heavily. "I've been living a lie, haven't I? My memories aren't even real. I'm no better than a computer programmed to do simple tasks, and I didn't even question any of it." He ran a hand through his hair. "How could I not question things?"

"I don't know. I'm not an expert on curses. Heck, I've never encountered anyone who's been cursed. "If you ask me, even if you did question something, I think once you awoke the next day, your doubts would've most likely been erased."

He pointed toward the door to the antiquities in the other room. "I'm no better than those objects I guard.

It's why I can enter the museum. I'm a preternatural being. I'm also enchanted like a person in a demented fairy tale, but I have a hunch no one's going to kiss me awake."

Her brows rose. He knew about fairy tales? He sure was full of surprises.

He met her gaze, and she had the urge to wrap her arms around him and tell him it would be all right, but she couldn't. It may never be all right for him. She settled on resting her hand on his shoulders. "We're going to make this better, I promise." In a sense, hadn't she already helped? Until today, Nerdy Darrien hadn't known of his other existence, and tonight, she would update Beastie Darrien.

"I wish I didn't know," he said.

His words made her heart drop a beat. "What do you mean?" she asked and feared she already knew the answer.

"The cruel joke is on me. I'll never do more than waste away in this place." He strode away from her and headed for the coffeepot on the counter.

She didn't know what to say. A moment ago, she congratulated herself with a job well done when all she'd accomplished was to make Darrien's existence a million times more daunting. "I'm sorry." Of course, the words fell short, and Darrien didn't respond other than pursing his lips.

For a moment, they stood there listening to the melody of the coffeepot gurgling and hissing its tune as it brewed. The rich aroma filled the air and her mouth watered for a taste despite the dire circumstances.

"It's not your fault," Darrien murmured at last, and then glanced her way. "I'm cursed, not dead." He straightened his shoulders and stood taller. "If a curse can be cast then there must be a way to undo it as well, yeah?" His glasses slipped, and he nudged them back on to the bridge of his nose.

He was definitely a trooper. She'd have to give him that. Perhaps she could see how Callista had fallen for such a guy. 'Cause if she were being honest here, she could do a little falling herself. She shifted her stance and cleared her throat. "Yeah," she answered him. "There has to be a way."

The coffeepot gurgling hit a crescendo before it tapered to a sputter then one last hiss for the finale. Darrien did the honors and poured two cups. She indulged with a careful sip and would have taken a more generous taste, but her cell phone vibrated. She lifted it from her back pocket and frowned as she caught sight of the caller ID.

"What's wrong?" Darrien asked, concern marring his features.

"It's Professor Leander."

"You shouldn't pick up," he said, panic lacing his words.

"I have to. I don't want her becoming suspicious." She was about to answer, but then on second thought, she put the call on speaker so Darrien could hear the conversation. Who knows, maybe he would detect something she hadn't from her previous conversations with the woman. "Hello," she said in greeting and hoped her voice sounded steady. Darrien stepped closer to her as if he were afraid he wouldn't be able to hear the professor from where he stood.

"Ah, Miss Angelis, you are awake," Professor Leander said, her voice rich with a hint of a Greek accent flavoring each word. "I'm calling to find out if you've had any luck acquiring the item we've chatted about. I must remind you that the deadline is fast approaching."

She didn't have to remind her. Calli could practically hear the tick-tock behind the call. "I'm working on it."

Silence on the other end greeted them, but then they heard the distinct tapping as if Professor Leander were drumming her fingers on a hard surface.

Calli glanced at Darrien. His eyes grew wider, and he lifted those broad shoulders in a shrug. She was at a loss wondering what Professor Leander pondered over. Finally, the woman graced them with an opinion. "Work faster, Miss Angelis." She ended the call with not so much as a goodbye.

"She's Greek," Darrien said, referring to her accent.

Calli slipped the phone back in her pocket. "Yes, so?"

"In Greek mythology, Leander drowned at sea, trying to reach the woman he loved."

"And this has to do with what exactly?"

He shook his head as if he hadn't realized he'd spoken out loud. "I don't know. You know when I told you I had a weird feeling of déjà vu from a gesture you displayed?" He didn't wait for her to answer but continued, "I had that same weird feeling when I heard Professor Leander's voice. Like I should know her. Like something as tragic as a man drowning at sea to reach his true love—that kind of feeling. Dread," he said the last word in a broken whisper.

Okay, can I say weird? However, she kept that

tidbit to herself because, let's face it, the last twelve hours had been a real trip down *Weird-As-Heck Lane*, and she really wanted to take another path. "Since you never leave the museum except to go to the grocery store, how is that possible? Because I highly doubt Professor Leander is shopping at your local grocery mart."

"I don't know," he said with all honesty. He removed his glasses and rubbed his eyes as if a headache throbbed behind his eyeballs.

"Let's see if we can find Professor Leander's photo on the Internet," she suggested. "Maybe if you see her face, something will trigger more of your memory."

"Good idea." He replaced his glasses on his nose. "But first I must call someone in to fix the window."

While Darrien made his calls, Calli sat at the computer and did a search for Professor Leander and her works. She could hear Darrien in the kitchen as he began calling a few repair shops. The first one he called must have been too expensive since his follow up exclamation was, "Bloody hell, this must be an elaborate jest on your part."

She looked over her shoulder at him standing in the archway, wearing an incredulous expression as he tried to negotiate a fair deal to repair the window. He turned and she stared at his broad shoulders and how they filled out his cardigan. His behind looked good in those very proper chinos he wore, too. The man was really something incredible to look at. On a sigh, she turned back to the computer. "Work before pleasure," she murmured.

Twenty minutes later, he finally strode back into the room. "The window repairman will be by in a couple of hours," he told her as he approached the desk.

She glanced over her shoulder. "By the way, I never apologized for breaking it. I hadn't wanted to damage the place."

"I'm surprised you didn't hurt yourself." He paused and then added, "You didn't, did you?" His brows furrowed over the bridge of his nose and his gaze wandered over her with concern.

"Surprisingly, no."

His features smoothed as he shook his head. "I'd say you must live a charmed life."

"Charmed? If so, I would have stolen the stone without a hitch."

"So, I'm a hitch, yeah?" He wagged his brows at her, and she chuckled at his sense of humor.

"You could say that. Come take a look here." She scooted the chair over so he could move in closer. "Here's a photo of Professor Leander." She pointed to the screen at a woman with her dark hair coiled into a bun. It had been difficult to find a photo of Professor Leander, at least one where Darrien could make out her features. She seemed to avoid the cameras, turning away as they shot the photo or lifting her purse to cover her face. This photo appeared to be a candid shot someone took without her realizing it. "Does she look familiar?"

"Hmm..." He leaned over her shoulder, so close she could turn her head and place a kiss on his cheek. She'd never dated anyone with a beard before. It tickled when he kissed her and she kind of liked it.

She shook her head as she chewed on her lower lip. She seriously had to rethink if she'd been hurt when she hurdled through the window. It would account for her mind wandering where it had no business going. It seemed the harder she fought the attraction to Darrien, the worse it became. Then she remembered when Beastie Darrien touched her hand in front of the motel room. The jolt of electricity had made her fly through the air and when she fell, she'd bumped her head. Her hand went to the base of her skull and her fingers gingerly felt for damage. She'd been knocked unconscious. Surely there had to be a bump and…there it was. She winced and Darrien's gaze riveted to her.

"Are you all right?"

Her hand fell to her side. "Yep, peachy." She almost grinned with relief. Her odd attraction to Darrien had nothing to do with curses and reincarnation or that he could kiss her senseless. A bump on the head had to be the explanation for her odd behavior.

He stood up straight then. "She looks familiar," he said about the photo of Mrs. Leander. "However, I don't know why. Let's see if there is anything else we can find out about her."

"Before I decided to take the job with her, I did some research, but didn't come up with anything to indicate she wasn't on the up and up. It was just my gut feeling making me hesitate."

His golden-brown eyes were truly beautiful, even with them shielded behind dark-rimmed glasses. "What did you say about hunches and inklings? Hmm?" He gave her a lopsided smile and didn't that just make him even more adorable.

She was doing it again, wasn't she? She let out a tired sigh and made an executive decision on her part before she did something stupid like tell him how adorable he was, and maybe even suggest they kiss just to see if they were compatible. Yep, she was losing it. Sleep deprived and a bump on the head could do that to a person. She frowned wondering if she should chance sleeping. She could have a concussion and—

"Calli? What's wrong?" Darrien asked.

Apparently he'd been talking to her for the last thirty seconds and she'd completely zoned out. "I'm sorry." She hastily stood to put some distance between them so she could breathe. But when her hasty departure from the chair seemed to increase Darrien's concern, he took a step toward her.

She lifted her hand to ward him away. Her heart pounded painfully hard, and she couldn't seem to catch her breath. "Is it hot in here?" she asked and pulled at her T-shirt.

"You're hyperventilating," Darrien told her. "You have to slow down your breathing or you'll pass out."

The room spun and she teetered on her feet.

"Calli," Darrien called to her and this time she couldn't keep him away. His hand snaked out to stop her fall, but the jolt of electricity that sizzled between them sparked to life once more. She shielded her eyes and cried out as the light, radiating around them blinded her.

Chapter Twelve

One moment Calli felt her body shutting down then the next second her body catapulted in another direction, somewhere else...somewhere foreign and yet familiar too. Had she passed out? Was this a dream or a vision? She blinked...and reopened her eyes, hoping to see the inside of the museum, but nothing changed.

****

She stood beneath the sky where the sun shone bright above, and in front of her the ocean glistened blue and green like sparkling diamonds. She could swear the scent of the sea tickled her nostrils. Never before had she experienced a vivid dream where she could decipher such succinct sensations.

The sound of giggling caught her attention, and she whirled to the right of her where footprints in the golden sand led to rocks up ahead. Curious, she followed them.

As she neared, she could make out voices, cheerful banter and teasing. Her trek led her to the other side of the rugged terrain to find a group of young people gathered as they enjoyed the sun and food spread out on a blanket.

Her gaze took in each face with interest. They were young, teenagers and seemingly friends. There were three boys and two girls. She studied their faces but paused when she realized one of the boys was Darrien, a very young Darrien as a teen, before he'd reached his full height. His face was void of lines brought on by heartache and years of isolation. This was a happier time for him, before the curse, before he'd lost his wife. Her attention shifted with interest to the girl beside him. She bore a striking resemblance to herself, so much so it made the hairs on her arm stand up on end.

"Callista," she breathed. This was the woman Darrien had loved. She strode closer, confident no one could see her. This was her vision quest, or whatever it was. She was an observer and nothing more.

Callista wore a brightly colored peplos, with a gold belt decorated with jewels. An emerald brooch pinned at her right shoulder finished off the outfit. Elaborate braids decorated her hair in a flattering style to keep the long strands away from her face. Darrien leaned over and whispered something in her ear. She pulled back with a laugh then jumped to her feet at a gallop. Darrien gave chase, and Callista giggled as she ran away—not too fast, making it obvious she wanted to be caught.

His hand snaked out and grabbed Callista's arm, bringing her to a halt. Her lips curved into a grin as he pulled her into a lover's embrace. The way they gazed at each other was as if no one else existed on the beach. What she wouldn't do to have someone gaze at her in such a way. Loved as if nothing else mattered.

A girl's scream penetrated the air, and the moment was lost as the two lovers parted in alarm.

Darrien looked toward the ocean, and Calli followed his line of vision. Had someone screamed from the water? A cry for help came again and this time Calli spotted someone adrift, with hands frantically waving in the air. Darrien glanced at Callista with a few words. She nodded and Darrien broke into a full run toward the water. He never paused his stride as he dove into the waves. In the matter of seconds, he broke the surface where the girl still struggled to keep her head above the water.

Calli breathed a sigh of relief when she saw Darrien had the girl and was making his way back to the shore. The others had gathered and Callista offered a cloak to put around the girl, who appeared to be a few years younger than the rest of the group. If Calli guessed, the child was no more than twelve or thirteen.

Something seemed oddly familiar about the girl Darrien had saved, but Calli couldn't quite put her finger on why. Dark straight hair plastered the girl's face, but she brushed it aside to peer up at Darrien with nothing short of hero worship.

"What were you doing out there?" Darrien asked the girl.

It took Calli a moment to realize they weren't speaking English, but Greek, or rather a similar dialect, and she could understand them perfectly.

"You know the waters are treacherous this time of day, Isa" he reprimanded her further.

Isa? She regarded the child curiously. The girl Darrien saved was Isa. She was tall, but all gangly limbs. This child would one day be the cold-blooded killer who took Callista's life? The girl's lips chattered, and her eyes were wide with fear. It made it difficult to believe such innocence could turn into something so hateful.

Isa's lips pouted and she looked as if she would burst into tears. "I'm sorry," she said between chattering teeth. "The water looked so inviting, and I couldn't resist." Then she did sob big tears, and her chest heaved as she tried to draw in a breath.

Darrien didn't seem to know what to do with a weeping child. Finally, he just pulled her into an embrace and patted her back. "It is all right. You are safe." He held her as he would a little sister, giving her comfort and naught else, but Calli could see something else in Isa's face as she rested her chin on his shoulder. She thought the embrace meant more. Her tears dried almost instantly, and her arms went around him as if she relished the feel of him against her.

A niggling in the back of her mind made Calli wonder if Isa had truly been in trouble or if the girl had planned the whole fiasco just to see if Darrien would come to her rescue. No, she wouldn't have, would she?

Isa's lips began to curve like a satisfied cat. "You really do care for me," Isa said, but Calli knew she meant more to that statement.

"Of course I care for you," he answered and pulled away so he could look at her. "Don't scare me like that again."

"No, never," she said and threw herself into his arms once more.

Calli glanced at the others who were there, but they didn't seem to notice Isa had designs on Darrien. Even Callista didn't seem fazed that the girl hung onto Darrien as if he were her life support.

Calli wondered if she could see it because she already knew what Isa was capable of doing. At this time and place, Isa was only a child infatuated with a boy. Calli took a step to move closer, but the world around her shifted again, and she found herself in another place and time.

This time Isa was following Darrien, who was with

friends his own age, but he didn't seem to mind having Isa tag along.

"I'll race you to the top of the mountain," one of the boys with a crop of blond hair announced to the group.

"I don't know," Darrien shook his head and jabbed a thumb in Isa's direction. "I don't think she'll be able to keep up."

Calli could tell he was teasing, but Isa's face scrunched up and she stamped her foot.

"Can too keep up. I can fly faster than any of you."

"Is that so?" Darrien's face broke into a grin. He glanced at his buddies. "What do you say, my friends, should we put it to the test?"

"We'll give you a head start, Isa," the brown-haired boy told her. "Seeing as you're a few years younger than we are. It's only fair." He brushed his hair back from his brow. Once Isa glanced his way, his face flushed red.

Calli had a hunch this boy was smitten with Isa, but she didn't seem to notice. She only had eyes for Darrien.

"I can keep up with the best of you. I don't need a head start," Isa claimed.

"Well then—" Darrien began, but was interrupted.

"Darrien, wait up!" someone called to him.

Calli turned as the others did, too. Callista was in the distance waving to them.

"Her again," Isa said with a roll of her eyes. "Doesn't the mere human know she can't come with us? She can't fly."

Darrien glanced at her with a chuckle. "She can fly if she's on my back." He jogged to meet Callista halfway, leaving Isa to stare after him, crestfallen that he chose Callista over her.

"Be glad, Isa," the brown-haired boy said. "You're sure to beat Darrien now, if he's carrying Callista. She may be petite, but she is still extra weight."

She threw the boy a disgruntled look. "I don't want her to come with us. She's not of our tribe."

"Darrien likes her," the blond boy said. "And besides, Callista is nice. She makes the best sweets."

Again Isa grumbled and started walking away with her head down.

"Hey, little one, where are you off to?" Darrien called after Isa, as he approached the group with Callista on his arm.

"You don't want me tagging along," Isa grumbled without turning around.

Darrien frowned but called after her. "Of course I do."

Isa halted her steps and glanced over her shoulder. Her gaze seemed to lock onto where Darrien's hand rested on Callista's arm. Isa's features hardened. "I don't want to play your silly game of who can fly the fastest." This time when she turned away, she didn't look back.

"I don't believe she likes me," Callista said.

Darrien laughed it off and gave her a kiss. "What's not to like about you? You're funny."

"And you're beautiful," the brown-haired boy spoke up with a smile.

"And you make us treats," the blond-haired boy added, which won him a slap on the back by the brown-haired boy.

"Is that all you think about? You're stomach?

"I'm a growing gryphon, of course I do," the brown-haired boy replied.

Calli turned to see where Isa had gone. She stood high above them, gazing down at Darrien and Callista.

Calli frowned as her gaze caught sight of Isa's eyes glimmering like gold, not in disappointment but in fury.

Again the landscape changed, and it took her a moment to regain her footing. These visions were taking a toll on her, and her stomach rolled to bring home the point.

This time she was indoors. Whitewalls of a Greek style villa decorated with mosaics and wall paintings met her gaze.

"There you are."

She whirled around at the sound of a deep rumbling voice of good cheer and was surprised to find Darrien standing in the archway, tall and sure and good looking as ever. She opened her mouth to speak, but before she could utter a word, a female voice answered him. With surprise her gaze riveted to the right. She hadn't noticed anyone else in the room with her.

Callista sauntered by her with graceful steps. She was no longer a young girl, but a woman, probably close to Calli's age. Up close, the resemblance between them was uncanny.

"What took you so long?" Callista said to Darrien and her lips curved as she walked into his embrace. Callista wore a rich colored, floor-length peplos. Surprisingly, no shoes adorned her feet. Elegant smooth toes peeked out from beneath her gown.

Darrien sported a dark blue chiton, red cloak, and sandals adorned his feet, an outfit similar to the one she saw Beastie Darrien wearing when she first met him.

"There has been trouble," Darrien told her. "A thief stole from the treasury, and I must go after him."

Disappointment marred Callista's features. "I wish your duties did not take you away this night. I have news of my own, sweet husband." Her hand caressed his cheek, and he leaned into her palm. "Though, my announcement is not so daunting."

"And what is it you wish to share? You have my full attention."

She sighed. "I wanted to tell you over a late-night meal, but I am bursting with happiness and cannot wait. I am with child." Her hand went to her flat stomach as if the evidence could be seen.

"She's pregnant?" Calli shouted in disbelief. Thank goodness, neither Darrien nor Callista could hear her.

Darrien was all smiles as he lifted Callista off her feet and swung her around. She giggled with delight, though she protested. "Put me down."

He did, but he didn't release her completely. Darrien leaned toward her and kissed her with a searing caress making Calli blush and turn away.

As their murmurs and breathing became more labored with passion, she felt her cheeks burn. and hoped she would be released from this dream… vision… or whatever the hell it was before she was forced to endure the couple's lovemaking.

A shadow crossed over her, making her glance toward the window. A figure of a woman stood there watching the two lovers, but Calli couldn't make out any features with the way the shadows played across the woman's face. Calli stepped closer to chance a better look and gasped in surprise. It was Isa, only older, and now she knew why Isa had looked so familiar when she was a child.

****

In the next second, Calli's wish to return to the present took hold and the world where Callista and Darrien were faded away. The museum's dark foreboding interior came into focus, as did Nerdy Darrien's worried features.

It took her a moment to realize why he appeared to be floating above her. She was lying on the ground, and he was fanning a folded paper at her as if the cool breeze would make everything all right. She slapped his hand away. "Stop that." She sat up, but the movement made her woozy.

"You fainted," he spoke the obvious just in case she hadn't figured out why she was taking a nap on the floor of the museum.

What was with this man and his electric zaps? Another thing that Nerdy Darrien and Beastie Darrien had in common. "I didn't faint," she lied. What a pair they both were. He was obviously a bad influence since she'd never swooned in her life before she met him.

"If you insist," Darrien said and sat down beside her so he faced her. "You had me worried," he told her.

Her gaze met his. Worry marred his features, and his skin had turned dead white. "I'm okay," she reassured him, even if she wasn't all that sure it was the truth. She rubbed her temple where a headache had started to take root. She'd dreamt of Darrien and Callista, but it didn't seem like a dream. It felt so real. "I had flashbacks of Callista and Darrien's life," she told him. "You know, before the curse."

"You did? Well, of course you did. You wouldn't have said so if you hadn't," he rambled on.

101

She placed a hand on his knee to get his attention. It worked. He immediately stopped talking as he stared at where her hand rested. She smiled and patted him once before she placed her hand in her lap.

"Callista was pregnant," she announced. "And… Oh, this is ridiculous." Voicing it out loud made her wonder how she could have believed the visions.

"Callista was pregnant?" he questioned more to himself, and his brows furrowed. "This would have been my child, then. Yeah?"

God, she was an insensitive jerk. Real or not, the stories meant something to him. "I'm sorry. It was just a dream." At least she hoped it was, but how would she come up with such stories? "I shouldn't have said anything." She scrambled to her feet and Darrien followed suit.

"What if it wasn't?" he asked. "I felt the shock between us when we touched. Skin to skin," he verified, "and when we shook hands before, too. You said last night my alter ego also shocked you. Maybe it's not so nutty you've had a vision. Maybe the electrical shocks are triggering memories and emotions to resurface from your subconscious."

She ran a hand over her face, feeling suddenly drained. Any other time she would have said *no way*, but too much had happened not to consider the possibility. "If that's the case, then I think we have a big problem. Professor Leander, or rather her *doppelganger* was there in my vision, too. She didn't look like she cared for either you or Callista."

Calli couldn't wrap her head around being Callista reincarnated, so she stuck with keeping their identities separate, for now.

"Could Professor Leander possibly be Isa then?" he asked. His gaze met hers as he spoke the question.

"What? Do you mean is she reincarnated or still alive?" A niggling at the back of her neck put Calli on edge. "How long do you suppose gryphons live? Not counting you since the whole cursed issue may play a part in your longevity."

"I haven't a clue." He shook his head. "There's not very much written about gryphons. Scattered through the centuries, there's only a mention of them here and there, but nothing substantial."

"Hmm. Well then, if Professor Leander is truly Isa—God, this just keeps getting better and better. Why does she want the stone…besides the obvious? I know it can control the dead. Even if I want to deny all the reincarnation mumbo jumbo, Professor Leander's involvement can't be a coincidence, and I can't help but think we're missing something vitally important. She's going to use the stone and it must have something to do with all of us and the past."

Despite all the excitement and the mystery to be solved, she yawned, quickly covering her mouth with a hand. "Excuse me. I'd like to hash this all out right now, but I'm going to be useless if I don't get some shut-eye. I need to go back to the motel for a few hours. I promise I'll return before the sun sets," she added.

"Of course. I understand." He nodded. "I'll see what else I can find out about Professor Leander. I'll also check the records we have on Hecate's Stone. Documents always arrive with the items, and I keep them in a file in the back. The book you glanced at only highlights the items, and as new ones arrive, the curator in charge is responsible for jotting down a brief synopsis." His brows furrowed. "I guess I'm the one responsible for all the information." He shook his head. "Just another thing I didn't realize. My memories tell me I only started working at the museum six months ago. Obviously, another lie to add to the many."

Her heart went out to him, but she could think of nothing to comfort him. She reached for him, and he placed his hand over hers with a pat.

"Well then," he said and let his hand fall to his side as he turned away. He strode over to the desk and moved items around as if he were looking for something. "I'll ring you if I find anything on the Internet about the professor," he said, "but I'll need a number where I can reach you. Now where is that pen?"

She strode over to the desk, shaking her head as her fingers nabbed a pen from the pencil holder. She lifted a post-it and jotted down her cell phone number. "There." She tapped the paper.

His lips curved at the ends as he slipped the note in the pocket of his sweater.

"I might as well have the number for the museum handy," she said. Her hand slipped into her pocket and produced her cell phone. He rattled off the number and she typed. Once she was finished, she tested the number out.

A half a second later, the phone rang, and Darrien sighed in relief.

"Looks like the number is legit then," Darrien said and met her gaze with meaning.

They just stood there staring at each other as if there should be more to say, but she didn't want to cross over any more lines she'd soon regret. The attraction between them still sizzled, but at least after her vision quest, she seemed more in control. She just wished her heart would stop doing handsprings in her chest every time he looked at her.

He cleared his throat. Maybe he was having the same difficulties. "I should get busy, yeah?" To prove his point, he took a seat and went to work on the computer keyboard, already zoning her out.

"Darrien?"

"Hmm?" he said without glancing her way.

"Thank you."

This made him look at her above the rim of his glasses. "It is I who should be grateful." His lips curved, and she couldn't stop herself from remembering those very lips pressed to hers.

Just the thought made her stomach flip-flop in anticipation of sampling him again. Then she remembered her vision and the love Darrien had for Callista...for her.

She squeezed her eyes shut. "I need to sleep." She quickly turned on her heels and strode toward the front door. "Don't forget someone will be by to fix the window," she called to him without breaking stride. Nerdy Darrien seemed to get easily distracted, and she didn't want him to be startled when the repairman made an appearance.

"Right-o," he called back.

Calli smiled at his response, she pushed the front door open, and stepped outside. She squinted at the brightness but welcomed the sun's rays warm on her face. Her gaze took in the empty parking lot and in the distance the vast vegetation. They were really out in nowhere land. Darrien had it right. How did Professor

Leander know about the museum? More, what was her end game with all this?

A light glinted on something in the distance, and she strode toward it to investigate. "I'll be," she murmured as she bent down and retrieved the dagger she'd thrown at the gryphon… a half chuckle escaped her. "Darrien," she corrected. Lucky for him he could turn to ether and avoid lethal weapons hitting their mark. She slipped it into its sheath attached to her belt.

After the night she'd had, she wondered what the day would throw at her. "Bring it on," she said to the heavens. She had a gryphon on her side. "What could go wrong?" She frowned wondering why in the world she'd voiced those words? Those words were always the kiss of death. Things usually went wrong when one thought they couldn't. "Crap. Double crap on a stick," she cursed, and her hand went to her necklace her father had given her. She lifted it to her lips and kissed it for good luck. She had a hunch they were going to need it. With a sigh, she turned and headed for her vehicle trying to shake off the unease of impending doom.

Chapter Thirteen

Darrien put in another call for a glass repairman when the first one never showed. It was already past one in the afternoon, and he was sure they would need more than a few hours to finish the job. He highly doubted his other more aggressive side would appreciate awakening to unexpected visitors. There was no telling what would happen then.

Calli explained how the window had been shattered, but he still had a difficult time wrapping his mind around the idea that a fight took place inside the museum, and she had to jump out the window to escape. It sounded like a very bad sci-fi movie, and he'd somehow been involved.

Sure, he had the build to do considerable damage, but good heavens he wouldn't intentionally try to harm someone. He shied away from the sight of blood. He'd cut his fingers plenty of times chopping vegetables and nearly passed out. "Dear me, I am a fainter." He pursed his lips, not liking the way he viewed himself.

He chanced a look at the gryphon staring down at him. "What are you looking at?" he snarled at the thing. "I bet I'd be a disappointment to you, wouldn't I? And I'm talking to a statue. Bloody terrific." Besides, if he were to believe all Calli had told him, the gryphon didn't even know about him. "Yeah, I have one up on you. What do you say about that?"

"Hello?" a male voice called from the broken

window.

He pushed away from the desk, the chair sliding on its wheels and giving him the space he needed to fly to his feet. His hand went to his tie and pulled on it to loosen it. "What do you want?" he asked and couldn't quite keep the apprehension out of his voice.

"I'm here about the window?" the man stated, like a question as he pointed to the open space in front of him. "I knocked on the door, but no one answered."

Darrien's gaze took in the work uniform and tool belt strapped to the man's waist and realized what he said rang true. "Right-o. Go on then. Fix away. The door is unlocked."

The guy gave him a nod. "Sure thing, boss." The repairman came around to the door and let himself in. He weaved around a rocking horse, and a table displaying jack-in-the-boxes, all cursed and with one of the boxes housing a ghost.

"Make sure you don't touch anything," Darrien warned the guy.

The man turned to look at him again. "No boss, just the window." He shook his head as he strode the remainder of the way to the window without incident.

Darrien sat down again and glanced at the screen on the computer. He'd found a site dedicated to gryphon lore with photos of winged-beasties, some hideous and others as majestic as the gryphon statue standing before him. Most of the articles listed the same information with only a few minor differences. One site spoke about how gryphons were like dragons. They both protected treasures. If a thief tried to steal something, the gryphon would capture the thief, but it would not kill him—at least, not at first. No, the beastie would ask the thief a question and if the thief answered correctly, he was set free with his prize in hand. However, if the thief answered incorrectly, he would die.

Darrien swallowed the lump in his throat. He really needed to concentrate on finding information about the woman who hired Calli, but how could he not be curious about what he was supposed to be? He glanced toward the worker and frowned when he found the man eyeing him before he quickly turned away and concentrated on the window once more.

Darrien shifted in his seat, and it creaked beneath his weight. "How's it going then?" he shouted to the repairman.

"It's coming along," the fellow called back without looking up.

Once the man went on his merry way, Darrien would feel better. His nerves were on edge, and he didn't need the distraction of worrying about someone in the museum accidently touching something they shouldn't. Really, couldn't the man fix the glass from the outside? He was about to suggest it, but the phone rang on his desk. He couldn't remember the last time he'd received a call. However, Calli opened a whole new world of wonder, and he started questioning everything. He believed he had a home in the city, but the image of the apartment was starting to fade. It was as if Calli had downloaded a virus in his brain by showing him the video of his change. Now the fantasy that the curse had created for his reality was diminishing as if the cobwebs of deceit were being brushed away. He glanced at the paper on his desk. He'd made two columns. One column was for what was real and the other for what the curse had fabricated.

Rrrr…ring ring…rrr ringring.

"Apartment—not real." He jotted it down then glanced at the other column. He had sci-fi movies, books, and different foods he enjoyed listed in the real column. Looked like the curse couldn't take away everything. Those memories remained vivid.

He was distracted from his thoughts when his stomach grumbled almost as loud as the phone's trill. Morning slipped into afternoon without him even realizing it. He should make himself a sandwich, and he noticed there was a bag of potato chips in the pantry.

Rrrr…ring ring…rrr ringring. The trill of the phone interrupted his thoughts yet again. "Phone," he said and grabbed for the receiver before the person calling hung up.

Silence met his ear, and he pulled the receiver away and stared at it.

"Hello? Darrien?" Calli's voice rang through, and he placed the phone back to his ear again.

"I'm here." Guess he should have said hello first, but he'd been too intrigued with the thought of someone phoning, to adhere to protocol.

"I'm on my way back to the museum," she told him, "but I'm stopping off at a drive-thru. Want something to eat?"

His stomach grumbled, deciding the answer. "If you don't mind, and I'll have whatever you're having."

"Sure," she said, and he could hear it in her voice how she thought his request peculiar.

He glanced at the worker, who'd been staring at him again, only to look away when he was caught. He whispered into the phone. "I've only eaten what's here in the museum…I think. Well, quite honestly, I can't recall stepping out to have fast food."

There was a long pause. "But you know of such places?" she asked.

"Just another thing to add to the pile of *how-do-I-know* when I never leave the museum." He couldn't quite keep the terseness out of his voice.

"Well, sit tight," she said. "I'll be there in a jiffy to give you a taste of home from your expert vagabond." He could hear the smile in her voice.

"I look forward to the experience." After saying goodbye, he replaced the receiver and stared at the phone with what he was sure was a silly grin. Calli would be here soon, and his smile slipped. He had nothing to show her.

He'd been making lists and looking up gryphon nonsense and not concentrating on Professor Leander. "Bollocks." He scooted the chair closer to the desk before his fingertips grazed the keyboard. He typed in Professor Leander but forgot to remove gryphon from his last search. Before he could correct his mistake, he was too quick, and his finger hit return. Once the screen refreshed, he was about to type in the correct search word but halted his attempt when something interesting caught his eye.

Professor Leander spoke at various universities regarding ancient Greece, her expertise and knowledge on the subject extensive, but what caught his attention was the topic she spoke about at a seminar in Arizona a few months ago. The title was Gryphons: Real or Myth? He clicked on the article.

"Professor Risa Leander," he read and paused. "Risa?" Drop the r and her name would be Isa. It was the first time an article stated her given name. Maybe this article would prove to be the connection they were looking for. Calli may have had a glimpse of the past, or she could have just blacked out and dreamt the whole thing. He glanced at the gryphon and grumbled, "Bet you'd know if this was really the Isa who caused this pickle we're in." Then he rolled his eyes when he realized he was again talking to the statue. He concentrated on the screen. Noticing the video to the right of the article, he clicked on the play button.

Professor Risa Leander appeared on the screen looking all prim and proper in her suit. Her hair was pulled back in a bun, apparently the only way she wore it. Her birdlike features weren't unappealing, but there was something about the woman he didn't like—a funny reaction if he didn't know her.

"The gryphon," Professor Leander began, "is considered a legendary creature by most. The creature possesses the body, tail, and back legs of a lion, with a head, wings, and talons of an eagle. The lion is considered the king of beasts and the eagle the king of the birds. A gryphon in legends and mythology was a majestic and powerful creature of both land and air. They were the guardians of treasures, priceless artifacts and possessions, and they were sought after to keep the possessions safe."

The woman spoke with passion as if she paid reverence to the creatures, and maybe there was a good reason for it. If Calli's vision could be trusted the professor was one such creature.

"Gryphons are depicted in the art and lore of Ancient Greece," Professor Leander continued, "and I am here today to argue the fact these creatures truly existed and were not legends of old, but they truly walked the earth."

"What?" he said and sat up straight in his chair. He wasn't the only one surprised by her outright claim. The audience expressed their astonishment as well.

"Quiet, please. You will all have your chance to voice your questions," she said, trying to silence the room.

If he didn't know better, he'd say the woman was a nutter, but after what he learned today, he would bet she did have proof. He pointed to the gryphon statue then to the computer as if the darn thing should pay attention too. "Are you hearing this?"

"Excuse me—"

"Bloody hell!" He jumped at the sound of the workman's voice and his heart slammed into his ribcage. He hadn't even heard the man approach, but he stood at the side of the desk peering at him with a smirk. "Don't sneak up on a bloke," he told the repairman.

Professor Leander's voice droned on in the background, and the repairman glanced at the computer screen. Flustered, Darrien tried to turn the video off and ended up hitting the volume before his third attempt did the job. He turned back to the repairman. "What is it then?"

"Didn't mean to startle you." The man's lips twitched as if he thought it funny he'd scared him half to death.

"Well?" Darrien asked, hoping the man would say what he wanted and go.

"I have the window measured and the area cleaned out. I'll be back in about an hour to install the glass.

You'll still be here, right?"

"Well, I'll have to be, now won't I?" he snapped.

The workman nodded, ignoring his poor attitude. "Good." He turned on his heel and headed for the door as Calli strode in, carrying lunch in paper bags.

His stomach rumbled in anticipation. "Down boy." He patted his stomach.

As Calli strode past the workman, she turned to give him a second glance, her brows knitting together. When she reached Darrien, she handed him a bag and kept the other.

"I thought the window would be fixed long before now," she said. "Is there a problem?"

"The first bloke didn't even show. This one's been here all afternoon. Annoyingly so."

"Where's he going? I still see a hole in the wall."

Darrien dug his hand into the paper bag to retrieve his lunch. He ripped open the wrapper revealing a juicy hamburger. He took a generous bite and sat back in his seat with a sigh. Pure bliss, he thought as he chewed. Surely if he ever had takeout like this, he'd remember it. Once he swallowed, he answered Calli's question. "He has to cut the glass. He'll be back later."

Calli stared at him with concern, but he didn't care. His stomach still demanded attention and he indulged in another healthy bite. As he chewed, his gaze slid over Calli with appreciation. It appeared she not only took a nap, but she'd showered too. Her hair was damp at the ends, making her ginger colored strands appear a dark auburn. As for her attire, gone were the formfitting black garments. They'd been replaced by jeans and a white blouse where her necklace lay nestled right above her modestly exposed cleavage. Just enough to entice, but not too much to make what lay beneath the silk obvious. Classy, he thought.

"Uh-hum," she cleared her throat, and he inwardly cringed. "Whatcha staring at, Darrien?"

"Uh, your necklace," he told her. He wasn't really lying. He'd been admiring it too.

"Okay, we'll go with that." Her lips curved, and he couldn't help but smile with her.

"It's an interesting piece," he said seriously. "Your necklace," he clarified and reached for a chip. Uhm-uh, French fries. The word popped into his head as he shoved one in his mouth. "Mmm-hmm. These are good."

"The necklace was a gift from my father," she told him.

"A talisman for protection," he said and reached for another fry, but ended up grabbing a handful instead.

"Yes," she said with surprise. "How'd you know that?"

"I like gems and stones, and not just the cursed ones." Then it dawned on him this was a true fact and not a fabricated one. He grabbed the pencil and jotted the info down in the appropriate column.

"What are you doing?" she asked and glanced at his list.

Warmth spread up his neck to his cheeks. "Making a list."

Her gaze met his with understanding. "Well then, you need to add a few things. May I?" She nodded toward the pencil, and he handed it to her. She turned the paper toward her. Once she was finished, her hand slid it back his way again. He read her clear script.

She'd written his name in the real column and hers below. His lips curved. He could become quite fond of this woman. He reached for the fry bag. There weren't many left.

"Here." She handed him her bag of fries with plenty left to savor. "I've never seen anyone enjoy French fries the way you do, or do you call them chips?" She chuckled.

"It's odd, don't you think?"

"What?" She joined him in sampling the fries.

"Why do I have a British accent when the museum is in the States?"

"You're cursed. Remember I told you Beastie Darrien said the museum moves every twenty years to a new location. You probably also spoke Greek at one time or another."

He was about to take another bite of his burger but lowered his hand. "How I wish I could speak to him." He nodded toward the statue. "He's more informed than I seem to be."

"You have all the human traits to fit in with society if someone approaches you during operating hours. He's more…"

"Beastie?" he offered.

"Not entirely true, but I sense he's more prone to slip into beastie mode. So, what did you find out while I was gone?" She was all business now.

"I almost forgot." He took the last bite of his burger before he focused on the computer. "I found Professor Leander online. She was at a seminar discussing if gryphons truly existed or not." He wiped his hands before he turned on the computer and found the piece for her.

Calli scooted closer to watch and her shoulder pressed against his. He could smell her perfume. Jasmine with a wee bit of vanilla. "Heavenly."

"What?" Calli asked with a start.

He cleared his throat and shifted in his seat. "Nothing. I…nothing." He ran a hand through his hair and tried not to melt into his seat at the way she stared at him, but she obviously wasn't going to let this go.

She turned his seat around so he was forced to face her, and he felt the warmth on his cheeks again. "I can't help it." He shrugged without being apologetic. "Do you have to be smart, interesting, and beautiful?" Her brows lifted and then he realized. "I spoke out loud, didn't I?" He groaned and closed his eyes.

"You did." She reached for his glasses, and his eyes opened wider as she removed them. She leaned forward and bloody well pressed her lips to his.

By the stars, he wasn't going to say no to her caress. He leaned forward and his hand went to her waist as he kissed her back. It felt liked he'd done this before, and not just when he'd fainted. Wait. He pulled back. "We've kissed."

"Yes," she said. "We were kissing…"

"I mean…not now." He knew he was making a muck of all this when her lips curved. "I meant to say, you've kissed him." He nodded toward the statue.

Still smiling, she leaned forward and kissed his forehead. "Relax. So I kissed Beastie Darrien. Well now, I've kissed you, too." She turned toward the computer as if kissing him and his alter ego was no big deal. She turned up the volume on Professor Leander's lecture.

Stunned at her nonchalant admission to kissing his

other half, his voice seemed to have solidified in his throat, leaving him speechless.

Chapter Fourteen

Calli purposely shifted mental gears. She didn't understand her attraction to Darrien...both Darriens. She didn't want to buy into the reincarnation thing. It was just too weird to think she'd been married and about to have a baby in another life. She'd barely dated in this one.

Nerdy Darien appeared just as confused as she was, leaving Beastie Darrien with the smug upper hand in the attraction department. Maybe curses sent out some kind of pheromone too powerful to resist. Yeah, gave the whole bad boy thing to the limit a clearer perspective.

"Could you turn up the volume?" she asked Darrien.

He moved the mouse over the icon. Professor Leander did have a lot of information regarding gryphons. It couldn't be a coincidence. Her thoughts brought her back to the vision. Was Professor Leander Isa? Were they one and the same person? If so, she'd be ancient. Calli glanced at the statue then to the man sitting beside her. He would be as old as Isa, and he was still alive. Just how long did gryphons live?

When the woman finished, another man took the podium thanking her for being the guest lecturer. Yadda, yadda, yadda. But then he went on to tell her how her findings were unfounded, and he remained unconvinced, and that the strange looking beast—his exact words—could never have existed.

"Whoa, no way!" Calli couldn't help laughing. "He probably shouldn't have insulted her." She studied Professor Leander's reaction. "Play it back," she told Darrien, waving her hand at the computer.

"All of it?" he asked in confusion as he sat forward to do as she asked.

"No, just the last few seconds."

He did.

"Right there," she said and couldn't keep the excitement out of her voice.

Darrien stared at her, obviously not getting it at all.

"Play it again but concentrate on her eyes."

Darrien did as she requested. "I'll be damned," he said in awe.

"There's our proof," Calli said. "She's a friggin' gryphon too." As she said the words, she realized what this meant. The vision she had was also probably real. She inhaled deeply as she let it all sink in. "Beastie Darrien said Isa killed his wife." She stood and paced. "So if Professor Leander is truly Isa, he'd know." She pointed to the statue. "We'll have to wait until he wakes. He'll confirm if it's her. Even if she's not, she's a gryphon."

Darrien continued to frown. "But what does she want? After all these centuries, why has she made herself known now?"

"I don't know." That part remained a mystery.

The door to the museum opened, and she turned to see the repairman who'd been there earlier with two guys flanking him.

"Where's the glass for the window?" Darrien murmured.

She had a bad feeling about this. Slow and easy she moved so not to alarm anyone, as she went for the gun in the holster clipped to her belt. Inside the waistband of her jeans, it was handily concealed beneath her blouse. Darrien's short intake of breath let her know he caught sight of what she was doing, but she couldn't worry about him now. These men meant business, and she had a hunch it wasn't the glass business.

She whipped the gun out. "Don't come any closer," she warned, already deciding the one in the middle would get it first if he even twitched the wrong way. He was the guy who had been there earlier and was most likely the leader of this soirée. She glanced at the nametag on his shirt that read Bert.

"What are you doing?" Darrien demanded beneath his breath, but he figured it out soon enough.

Bert grinned, and it wasn't an all nice and cozy kind of smile. In the next second, she knew why. His men were packing too, but with bigger guns.

"Put down your little toy," Bert ordered, referring to her weapon.

"You'll excuse me if I don't." She kept it locked on Bert with her finger on the trigger. "What do you want?"

"Only what was promised to Professor Leander. You didn't deliver the artifact," he said and waved for his men to lower their weapons.

She wasn't fooled. At a moment's notice, they'd be ready to shoot. "I have until October thirty-first. I don't know what calendar you boys use, but I still have plenty of time."

His lips curved. "We'll take the item now, if you please." He held out his hand as if she'd just plop the

121

stone in his palm and call it a day. "Professor Leander doesn't want you getting any ideas."

"And what ideas are those?" she asked. She didn't care to be backed into a corner and it looked like Professor Leander was pushy. Guess her phone call with her earlier gave the impression she was having those second thoughts.

"Just give it to him," Darrien said, loud enough for the thugs to hear.

"What?" she chanced a look at him then noticed his finger rested on a button beneath the desk. She didn't have time to contemplate what would happen when he pushed the button. He'd already made the decision for both of them. One second, she faced three thugs, the next she was free falling beneath the museum on a slide, listening to Darrien curse behind her. If they lived through this, she was going to kill him.

As the slide ended abruptly, she flew through the air for a brief moment before she landed hard on her rump. She rolled away, and not an instant too soon, since she believed Darrien ended up in a heap where she'd been seconds before, if the harrumph was any indication of where he'd landed. She couldn't see him as the lighting in the room proved non-existent.

"Where are we?" she asked, wondering if they were in an underground cave. She crawled to her feet, wondering where her gun went after she'd lost it in the fall.

There was a sound of a click to the right of her then light illuminated around them. Once her eyesight adjusted, she realized they were in what appeared to be a storage room with cases of food, water, ammo, and other goodies one might need in a dystopian situation.

If Isa got her hands on the stone, all this might come in handy with the impending threat of a zombie apocalypse.

"We're in an underground bunker," Darrien told her, as if having a bunker beneath a museum with an escape hatch was a normal thing. "I can add this to the real column," he said.

He hadn't been sure it was here before he pushed the button. They'd have to have a talk about him acting on his assumptions. "So there's an escape route, but what about the guys topside? Huh? Do you think they're just going to stand there and not try to find us? What's stopping them from taking a ride down the slide right now?"

"I had no other choices available. If you have not noticed, my cape is at the cleaners." His words dripped with sarcasm as he glanced at his attire before meeting her gaze with meaning. "Those were three armed men, if you hadn't discerned, and we only have one itsy-bitsy revolver between us. Please, do the math and tell me what you come up with."

"Well, if you put it that way…" She rather liked uppity Darrien. "But now we're trapped," she spoke the obvious. "What about the slide?"

"The buttons will not work a second time unless reset, and it has to be done from down here. We aren't trapped. The thugs are." He strode over to a monitor bolted to the wall on the far corner. He activated it and the screen revealed the museum above them. Two things hung from the ceiling, swaying back and forth like pendulums. It took her a moment, but then she realized it was two of the thugs, hanging by their feet. "There are a few buttons beneath my desk," he clarified. "I activated the trap at the same time I pushed the button for our escape.

"Where's the leader of the pack?" she asked with dread, not seeing him anywhere in sight.

He changed the screens on the monitor, activating other cameras in the room.

"I never noticed cameras in the museum," she said and stepped closer.

"You wouldn't have. Think of them as nanny cams strategically placed in each room. One is a tiny fly on a wall, another is a statue of Buddha, and yet another is a lion. The camera is located in its tail and the tail is mobile so I can see the entire room."

"Impressive, and I'd like to pick your brain on all this, but I'm worried about where Bert is." She really didn't want the guy running back to Professor Leander and telling her what went down. Heck, he could be calling her on his cell phone as they sat down here admiring nanny cams. "We have to go topside."

"Up there?" his voice rose and cracked.

"Do you have a better idea? We can't stay down here. It's only a matter of time before Bert figures out how to get to us. I want to have the advantage."

She whirled around in search of her gun and spotted it near the slide. She strode over to retrieve it then turned to face Darrien. He appeared none too pleased with her suggestion. "Listen, you can stay here," she told him. "I'll go up—"

"No, I'm coming with you." He stood up taller and inhaled deeply before letting his breath out in a whoosh. Glasses, cardigan, and attitude…check. He may not realize it yet, but he'd just donned that cape.

"Let's do it then," she told him, keeping her gun

ready. She glanced at the slide then to Darrien, hoping he knew of another way out of here. "Please tell me there's a door out of here?" She hadn't climbed up a slide since she was six years old and suspected the attempt wouldn't be nearly as much fun as she remembered.

"Right." Darrien strode to the opposite wall where a keypad was mounted. He entered a code then stood back. Deafening clanking noises filled the room as metal movements ground against each other. The wall beside the keypad began to open, revealing a steel door with another keypad beside it. There were no buttons, only a smooth surface. He used his thumb to activate the keypad. The lock mechanism clicked, and the door slid open, revealing a narrow hallway and stairs leading up. Lights mounted on the wall flickered to life with a buzz and snap of electricity revealing a hatch with an exit sign nailed above it at the top of the steep incline.

"The stairs lead outside to where the carport is located," he told her and led the way.

Once Darrien pried the door open at the top, he stepped through then leaned down to give her a hand up.

"Well, well what do we have here?" The deep voice boomed from around the dusty vehicle parked in the carport.

Darrien screamed and wrapped his arms around Calli in a bear hug, but just as quickly, he released her. "Sorry," he apologized and stood beside her and straightened his cardigan, probably hoping to regain his dignity.

"You weren't going to leave without saying goodbye, were you?" Bert asked. "It's too bad I was quicker than your traps inside the museum, huh?" He nodded with his head toward the building.

"Yeah, right. Too bad," Darrien murmured.

"Now drop your gun, Miss Angelis, or the nerd boy gets it."

She dropped it at her feet, which didn't please Bert in the least.

"Kick it toward me. Now!" he demanded.

She did what she was told, and Bert hunkered down to retrieve it while keeping his gun trained on them. Once he stood to his full height, he addressed her. "Now, I'll take the stone, Miss Angelis," he demanded with a wave of the gun, as if they could forget he could shoot them just for the heck of it.

"I don't have it on me," she told him.

His brows lifted. "Come now."

"No, it's true," she repeated. "Why would I carry the item on me and chance losing it? And look what happened today. The museum was held up by thugs." She gave him a cheesy grin then just as quickly pursed her lips.

He didn't appear pleased at her sarcasm. "You're a might cozy with the curator. Makes me wonder if you were cutting a deal with him."

"Him?" she said and jabbed her thumb in Darrien's direction. "He didn't even know I had the stone until now." She placed the back of her hand near her mouth and whispered, "Thanks for ratting me out." Truly, her mockery was lost on this guy. He only cared about the stone.

Bert glanced at Darrien who shrugged. "Don't look at me, mate. I don't know where it is."

"So why are you here then?" Bert demanded to

know.

"Isn't it obvious?" she asked with a girly chuckle. "I wanted some alone time with Darrien. A girl gets lonely on the road, if you know what I mean." She winked at Bert. "We were about to take our meeting to a more private setting until you barged in."

"We were?" Darrien's gaze riveted to her as he pulled at his collar. If they made it out of this alive, she was going to remove his tie and burn it.

"Yes," she said with meaning as she turned to give Darrien a wink, only he could see. She needed him to play along with this.

"I don't care how you get your jollies, Miss Angelis." Bert sneered. "I just want the stone."

She let out an exaggerated sigh as she glanced at Darrien. "We'll have to pick up where we started later, darling." She drew him nearer with one arm around his neck, as if she were about to give him a lip-lock from a girl madly in love...or the way she believed it was done. Truly, it proved easy to kiss Darrien. Passion seemed to spark between them whenever their lips touched, but now wasn't the time to indulge in such fantasies. Her hand palmed the pouch housing the stone from her pocket along with her cell phone. She then transferred the items into Darrien's pocket of his cardigan.

"Enough already," Bert snapped with annoyance. "You're coming with me, Miss Angelis."

She broke the kiss but didn't release Darrien right away. He appeared flustered from their embrace, and in truth she was a bit unsteady herself. "Darlin', you do know how to kiss," she murmured and ran a forefinger over his lips before she faced Bert.

"Go," he demanded of her as he waved the gun at her. She'd taken only a few steps when she noticed Bert raising his other hand. He held her gun in his grip and pointed it at Darrien. Then it dawned on her what he was about to do.

"No!" she cried, but he'd already pulled the trigger.

Chapter Fifteen

Darrien opened his eyes and blinked as he tried to recall why he was sprawled on the ground in the carport, but the pain radiating down his shoulder and back, made deciphering anything impossible.

"Think," he told himself and squeezed his eyes shut. He and Calli were in the museum... Thugs arrived with guns... Attempt to escape... Bert tried to stop them. He groaned as the fragmented moments came into sharp focus.

Where was Calli? He used his good arm to push himself into a sitting position, the jerky movements causing him to wince. He plopped back against the side of the building and swallowed back the nausea. Luckily, his glasses were still on or seeing would have been another drawback to this spectacular day. He adjusted them so they sat on the bridge of his nose and not lopsided off one ear. The carport immediately came into focus. "Much better." A quick survey told him Calli wasn't sharing his fate, but it still didn't tell him where she'd gone. She wouldn't have left him willingly. This much he could count on.

"Think...think, dammit!" The last thing he remembered was Calli kissing him... No, no after... Yes, he remembered. She was being forced to leave with the repairman, who obviously was not a real repairman, but someone who worked with Professor Leander. "The man shot me!" he exclaimed out loud and glanced down at where his hand lay over the wound, blood stained his cardigan and there was a ghastly hole in it. Since he wasn't dead, he had to assume the repairman missed his heart or anything else that might be essential to staying alive. Lucky him, he winced. Yeah, right.

"Calli, where are you?" he breathed with worry. She wouldn't be so lucky if she didn't cooperate, and he had a hunch she wouldn't. She was a stubborn woman, and her spunk would kill her, or it might just keep her alive. He scooted to his knees and tried to stand but the pain crippled him, and he fell back down. Gravel jabbed into his palms and knees, and the sudden jolt sent a shockwave of distress straight to his injured shoulder. "Bollocks," he cursed and squeezed his eyes shut as he rode out the pain.

He couldn't give up. Calli's life depended on him hauling himself back inside the museum and calling the police. Even as he thought this, he wasn't sure if the police would even believe the fantastic story of a cursed stone, thugs breaking in to steal it, and then kidnapping the original thief because they believed she had the hidden stone. "Bollocks," he said again with a hunch the word would soon become his favorite. No, he couldn't call the police. They'd probably arrest him for wrong-doing then search the desert for Calli's body, believing he'd done away with her.

There had to be something he could do, but maybe first he should take a gander at his wound. Even if he hatched a brilliant plan, it would be worthless if he bled to death.

He sat back down with a harrumph. He couldn't lift the injured arm, so he had to rely on his good one. He loosened his tie and pulled it over his head then he went to work on the buttons, his fingers fumbling to undo them. Finally, he managed to push the material to the side, further irritating the wound. He inhaled sharply and closed his eyes. Trying to breathe through his nose while he bit down on his lower lip, he mumbled, "Bloody, bloody, bloody…" Yeah, that really smarted. He wiped the sweat from his eyes with the back of his hand, no doubt spreading blood across his forehead. He chanced another look at the damage.

Blood pooled at the wound site, but it wasn't gushing. He shifted his weight and glanced over his shoulder for an exit wound. His skin remained unmarred. No exit wound meant the bullet was still lodged inside him. He was pretty sure that was a bad thing. Well, it couldn't be helped right now. Since the wound was only oozing, perhaps he wouldn't bleed out in the next few minutes. "Maybe when the sun sets the beastie will have a better chance at…" An idea sparked to life. Funny, how the fine edge of pain sharpened one's perceptions.

He scooted to his knees then braced himself against the wall as he attempted to stand. This time he remained on his feet, thinking as soon as his blurred vision cleared to at least a nice fuzzy haze, he would stumble his way back inside the museum. Yeah, anytime… Anytime… Yep, anytime… "Move, dammit," he told himself, and his pesky insistence seemed to motivate his feet into action.

Time proved a factor. At night, he would turn into his alter ego, stronger, more determined with the ability to hunt down the thieves. A particular thief, he corrected. The beastie would be able to find Calli.

Granted, he'd have to live long enough for the shift to occur then hopefully his alter ego would be strong enough to withstand a bullet wound. He had no way of knowing this for sure, but it was all he had.

He stared at the sky where the sun sat low on the horizon, painting it pink and purple with tinges of yellow. He'd been unconscious for a while. If the sun was going to set soon, that meant Calli had been gone for hours, too. She could be already dead. "No." He adamantly shook his head. No, he wouldn't believe it.

He hurried as fast as he could toward the front of the museum, stumbling and weaving like a drunken fool, but he managed to keep on his feet. The window still had not been fixed, which left the museum vulnerable, but it couldn't be helped. If a thief wanted to try his luck with a cursed item, good luck to him. The blimey bastards could take the fast track to hell for all he cared.

He pushed open the door and strode into the museum. The ropes which had once hung from the ceiling lay in piles of weaved hemp on the floor. Guess Bert cut down his buddies and took them with him.

His desk never seemed so far away. With each step he took, sweat rolled down his face and beneath his collar. He might as well be in the desert, trying to reach a mirage of an imaginary oasis as it slipped farther away with each step. He inhaled, taking in gasps of air and felt lightheaded. "Don't you dare pass out," he ordered himself, as if threats would defy the odds.

Unlike the endless desert, the museum didn't trick the eyes and conjure mirages. He finally stumbled to his desk, leaving bloody palm prints as he went. As he plopped down in the seat, his gaze caught sight of the massive gryphon sitting there staring with its lifeless stones for eyes. Calli believed the gryphon and he were one and the same, and her video proved the fanciful tale was the truth.

He pushed aside his cardigan and shirt once more to glance at the wound. It throbbed as if it had a heart of its own. His walk from the carport must have aggravated it. The blood poured more freely now. He opened a drawer at his desk and grabbed a handful of tissues from the box he kept in there. He pressed them to the wound, but the tissues turned red as the blood raced up the material and soaked it. He let his shirt fall over the wound once more. He would have to work fast before he passed out from lack of blood.

Calli's presence in his life had triggered something which had lain dormant inside of him. His capability to decipher what was real and what was fabricated. Now it was time to enlighten his other half.

He pursed his lips. A curse was meant to punish, condemn, or trap. He'd been subject to all three. His gaze shifted to the other cursed items in the museum. They all had a story and none of them ended with happily-ever-after.

He pushed back the glasses that had slid down his nose and grabbed for a pen and paper, praying the sun would set before he bled out. Calli pushed his destiny in another direction just by showing him the video. Maybe he could nudge his path a little more. He scribbled a note about what happened, hoping it would make sense to his other half, the gryphon half, his more aggressive half. Calli needed a badass right now, and who better than a creature that could tear the bad guys apart.

His hand paused over the paper as a fleeting

thought entered his mind. What if he died before the change took place? Would it be the end of the curse? The end of his existence?

Heck, he didn't know. Maybe all this summarizing could be a delusional trick from lack of blood. Maybe Calli didn't even exist. Maybe the thieves broke in and the job went sideways. He had been shot in the process, and his mind just made up the fantastic story of gryphon statues coming to life and saving the day.

He sat back in his seat and chuckled. "I'm the nutter, aren't I?" But then, he remembered Calli's sweet lips and knew he hadn't imagined the distinct warmth the memory conjured. She'd kissed him before the repairman shot him. He sat up straight, but the sudden movement had him seeing stars and he grabbed the desk to steady himself. "Bloody hell!" He waited for the wave of nausea to pass before he shoved his hand into his sweater pocket. Calli had put something there. Once his fingers clasped the items, he fished them out and placed them on the desk.

He blinked. "Mobile and …" he reached for the pouch and opened the drawstring to dump the object on the desk. "The stone." She'd given him the stone the thugs had wanted. His gaze shifted to the mobile and realized why she'd given it to him. He quickly grabbed another post-it and scribbled watch the video and placed it on the phone, but then took it off again. He would leave a personal message for his other half and tell him what happened while he slumbered. It took him a few minutes, but he managed to videotape a somewhat coherent rundown of what had happened. He placed the phone down and slapped the post-it on top of the screen.

His gaze slid to Hecate's Stone which Professor Leander wanted, and the damn thing stared back... Well, if it had eyes, it would have been staring back, but it did seem alive, pulsing with energy. His eyes narrowed as his vision blurred. He was going to pass out after all. Why was the stone glowing? His gaze landed on the blood smeared across it. "Blood would activate the stone... Bollocks, that can't be good." His head fell forward, bouncing on the desk. He was dying and for a moment he wondered if he'd come back to life as a zombie. "A zombie gryphon..." he murmured. A shiver of dread slid through his veins as that horrific thought took root.

Chapter Sixteen

The sound of traffic, and an occasional honking of a horn told Calli they were no longer in the outskirts of town. She didn't realize Professor Leander had an office in Arizona, but then she did own a corporation and told her she had numerous locations. Since she'd been spying on her, it made sense she'd be hovering close.

Once the van stopped moving, she scooted with her feet away from the door to the farthest point of the van. Her hands were tied behind her back, but they didn't bind her feet, and she wore steel-toe boots. The van door slid open, and Calli squinted against the light filtering in. It wasn't bright out, but the van didn't have any windows and she'd been in the dark for some time.

Bert's companion, the one with the long hair pulled back in a ponytail, stepped into the van. He reached down to grab her arm, and she let him have it right between the legs.

His strangled cry echoed in the vehicle, and he fell hard...on top of her. "Ugh!" The air went out of her in a whoosh when the full weight of the man hit her. She wasn't sure what hurt worse, her head being slammed against the panel, or her arms being smashed behind her. So much for that brilliant plan.

Bert stepped in to investigate. His hand whipped out to grab Mr. Ponytail and roll him away without a second glance. Then he turned his attention to her. His

136

hand snaked out, and he hauled her out of the van, none too gently. "If you try any funny business with me, Miss Angelis, I won't hesitate to show you how funny I can be." A knife materialized in his hand—long, pointed, and sharp. "The professor wants you alive, but she didn't specify what condition she expected when you arrived. Do I make myself clear?"

She swallowed back the lump in her throat and nodded.

"Good," he said and smiled. He wasn't a bad looking man if one was into thirty-something thugs with a mean streak. She was not.

"You know, smugness doesn't become you," she told him.

"And being a smartass doesn't become you, Miss Angelis. Now, let's go." He ushered her toward the high-rise made of glass and stone, impressive among the other brick and mortar buildings surrounding it. Her wrists were raw from trying to escape and the way Bert pulled on her arm made them hurt worse.

"Move it," Bert said when she tried to slow her steps. His fingers bit into her upper arm making her wince. She'd already decided the bastard would get it first for shooting Darrien. Making it happen couldn't come too soon.

Inside the building, they took the elevator, and she hadn't been overly surprised when he hit the button for the top floor. If Professor Leander was indeed a gryphon, and Calli was pretty sure she was, the woman would most likely want access to the roof so she could take flight with ease.

Ding…ding…ding…was the only sound in the elevator. Bert and his cohort didn't speak, but faced forward, waiting for the doors to open. She would have taken awful elevator music over the chimes of impending doom.

Finally, with a slight rise and fall motion, the elevator halted and the doors slid open. What do you know? Another ding. Bert nudged her forward, and they headed down a corridor brightly lit with overhead lights. Classical music played in the background. Now there was music? She rolled her eyes.

She admired the artwork on the walls and couldn't help but notice there was a large range of talent displayed. Renoir, Van Gogh, and Waterhouse just to name a few she recognized. The way the paintings were arranged was like walking into a museum of fine art.

They reached a door at the end of the hall and one of the thugs opened it for them. Bert motioned her to move ahead of him, but by no means did he risk letting go of her arm. Once inside, he shoved her in front of Professor Leander who sat behind a sleek, black desk.

Calli stumbled but managed not to fall on her face. She threw Bert a dirty look over her shoulder, letting him know how much she didn't like being pushed around. Then she leveled her gaze on the professor sitting queen-like in her throne of black-leather. Instead of a wall behind her, a large window appeared to open up to the heavens. Just how high up were they?

Professor Leander wore her dark hair in a tight bun, giving her eyes a slanted exotic appearance, and her makeup was polished with blush to give color to her cheeks. The professional getup—blouse, jacket, and possibly slacks or a skirt—she'd have to stand for Calli to know which. Whatever the case, the outfit made the professor appear as if she were a respected executive at a high-end paying job.

The paintings on the wall in the office were just as impressive as the ones in the corridor. Guess the stories about gryphons were true. They did like their treasures. Calli's gaze took in the rest of the room. Vases and sculptures were arranged strategically in curio cabinets and on display tables. A statue of a wizard stood guard on the left side of the desk, and an angel with wings carved to perfection stood guard in the corner to the right. A Doctor Who episode came to mind, and she shuddered at the thought of it. Would it move if she blinked? She shook her head. She really needed to cut down on her sci-fi addiction, but she couldn't help but chance another look at the statues. A chill ran down her spine, and she shivered. Definitely creepy.

"Well?" Professor Leander asked and her right eyebrow rose a fraction of an inch.

"Well what?" Calli asked as she focused her gaze on Professor Leander once more. She'd let Professor Uptight spell out what she wanted since she called this impromptu meeting.

"Don't play coy," the professor snapped. "I want Hecate's Stone. You were paid to retrieve it, and yet I still do not have it in my possession."

"Like I told your goons, I don't have the artifact on me, but they dragged me here anyway. And you only paid me half of what you owe me," she added for good measure.

Professor Leander drummed her long fingernails on the desktop as she stared at her for a millisecond longer before shifting her gaze to Bert. "Check her!" Professor Leander ordered Bert and he took a step toward her.

"Whoa, wait a minute." Calli backed away in protest. The last thing she wanted was Bert fondling her in search of something she didn't have. "I told you, I don't have it on me. It's back at the motel, but your goons wouldn't take me there. Said their orders were to bring me straight to you. And F-Y-I, I didn't sign up for murder."

Professor Leander's nostrils flared, truly not a flattering look for her with that uptight hairdo. Made her nose appear beaklike too. Maybe the gryphon side of her was lurking close to the surface.

"Murder?" Professor Leander asked. "What are you prattling on about?" She glanced at Bert.

His shoulders slumped, and he managed to look somewhat contrite. "I had to shoot the caretaker at the museum," Bert said. "He would have called the cops."

Professor Leander inhaled and exhaled deeply as if her temper wished to be unleashed. "I wanted the stone and the girl, dimwits," she said. "I never mentioned you should shoot the caretaker."

Calli blinked in surprise and had to close her mouth. Professor Leander didn't condone murder? Go figure. She didn't know the woman, but with the thugs she hired to do her dirty work, she would have thought eliminating a life here and there wouldn't bother her at all. Heck, if she were truly Isa, the woman staged her own murders.

Then it registered what Professor Leander had said. She wanted the stone and…the girl. Like in…she wanted her? Her body stiffened in automatic defense. "Why do you need me?" she blurted out before she could rein in her curiosity.

Professor Leander's lips curved. "Opening the

portal to the other side requires blood."

Calli swallowed hard. When the evildoer decided to share their plans, it usually meant the one hearing such tactics didn't live long enough to tell anyone else about it. Why did Isa need her blood? Wouldn't one of her goon's blood suffice? "So slice your own palm and go for it," she spat with more bravery than she felt.

Professor Leander didn't seem to find her suggestion useful, if her frown of displeasure was any indication. "You say the stone is at the motel?"

"Didn't I just tell you that?" she answered the question with a question.

"If you're lying, Miss Angelis, you will not like what I'll do to you. Take hold of her," she ordered Bert. "She's coming with us."

Before Calli could move, his hand snaked out, grabbing her upper arm in a grip that cut off her circulation, and adding pain to her back and wrists. She inhaled sharply and Bert chuckled low in his throat as if he enjoyed her discomfort. She really hated this guy.

Professor Leander stood and straightened her jacket. What do you know? The woman donned a skirt for her 'let's raise the dead' party. Her three-inch stilettos finished off the attire. She did have a striking figure—tall, graceful, and although not beautiful, she had a classical look. Unfortunately she was insane.

Her slanted eyes roved over Calli with renewed interest as she sauntered over to her. "You look like her, you know. Her hair was the same shade of dark copper as yours, and her eyes were like moss."

"What are you talking about?" Though, she already had a good idea, she was all about the proof and she'd like to hear Professor Leander say it.

"Callista," the professor said the name like the syllables burned her tongue. "Darrien's soul mate." If she could have spat on the floor and not appeared unladylike, Calli was sure Professor Leander would have done just that.

"What do you know of Darrien?" she asked, still pushing for confirmation that she was indeed the Isa from Darrien's past.

Her hand cupped Calli's chin. "Come now, sweet girl. Did you believe I came to hire you because of your credentials?" Her fingers squeezed her jaw before she shoved her back. She bounced off Bert's chest, who still had a hold of her arm.

Calli didn't answer the question but remained silent. Of course she'd wondered how the professor found her, but the woman was a great storyteller. She'd fabricated an elaborate lie with stories about how she'd known her father, and how they met at college. Calli located the transcripts, and the details the professor knew about her father were uncanny. Professor Leander may be a deceitful witch, but she was a thorough one.

"I've waited centuries for this moment," Professor Leander said as she glanced toward the large window as if reminiscing about her journey to this point in time.

Being this high up, the city was spread out before them, and the vehicles below looked no bigger than ants trailing behind each other as they headed toward their destination. At night, the city would come alive with color, but it wouldn't take away from the sky. The stars would twinkle above the city lights, and from this window it would be the perfect show.

"All the stars are aligned and of course," Professor Leander told her, "you're here." The woman met her gaze then. "I had to wait for Callista's soul to be reborn for all this to work to my advantage. You did take your sweet time, I must say."

As much as she'd like to refute the whole soul reincarnation business, she couldn't anymore. Not with all the weird things that had happened in the last day— gryphon shifters, visions, and Hecate's Stone that housed enough power to open a portal to the underworld.

Professor Leander was Isa. She didn't have to witness the woman going all beastie and spreading her wings to have it confirmed. She'd said enough to remove all doubts. She had waited centuries for this moment. Her words.

In Calli's visions, she'd witnessed how Isa was as a child. She'd always been jealous of Darrien and Callista's relationship, and in the last vision, Isa had stood outside the couples' window, coveting what she could never have. As much as Calli would like to believe those snippets were a true glimpse of the past, there were always two sides to a story. She'd have Isa's...even if it ended up being the perverted version. Villains always believed they were justified when they performed their heinous acts.

"Let's say I'm Callista reincarnated," Calli began, "who the hell are you in this never-ending saga?"

Professor Leander's chuckle was more a courtesy laugh. "I'm Isa, and don't try to deny you didn't already figure this out. I know how chummy you were with Darrien at the museum. Heads together and scheming, no doubt." She paused as if waiting for Calli to confirm or deny her claims. When none came, she sighed and shook her head. "Darrien was to be mine, but the fool always had a fondness for the human side of his existence. Gryphons mate for life. Did you know that? Gryphons," she said again, this time stressing the importance of that one word. "Not humans and gryphons. Humans don't know the first thing about having a life commitment. They throw their love away on the first person who pays attention to them." Her hatred for humans radiated off her like heat from a furnace, her face turning redder and redder as she voiced her grievances against the human race.

Now she got it. Isa wasn't into the whole multi-cultural marriage thing. She supposed this applied to preternatural beings as well. So she didn't believe it possible for Darrien to find his true love with anyone other than another gryphon shifter. "You said Darrien was to be yours. Why did you believe this? Did he tell you he wanted to be with you? Did he proclaim his love for you?"

Isa's eyes narrowed. "He didn't have to. He told me with his actions. He was always there for me and would never let anything bad happen to me. He always made sure to include me when he was off to have an adventure. We were inseparable when we were children."

The way she described it made it sound like they were best buddies. "Just you and him…together, right?" she asked, knowing full well Darrien and Isa had not been alone when these so-called adventures took place. Isa conveniently forgot Darrien had many friends and didn't exclude anyone, including a child who wanted to tag along.

Isa waved her hand. "Some of the others in our tribe would join us, now and again. But Callista always butted in when no one cared to have her around. She couldn't fly like the rest of us. She always slowed us down, but Darrien was too kind to leave her behind and would volunteer to let her ride on his back. She tricked him into falling for her. It was all a ploy to keep him away from me."

Calli pitied Isa in a way. Isa hadn't understood Darrien cared for her as he would a little sister. She misconstrued every act of kindness as something more. If only Darrien had realized Isa's infatuation had turned to something more sinister, he might have been able to reason with her. "So what did you do about Callista stealing Darrien away from you?" she goaded, wanting her to confess.

Isa harrumphed. "I couldn't believe he actually married her. It was true a few of the others from our tribe had taken human mates, but Darrien was a warrior, respected among our members. He could have one day been a great leader of our tribe. He'd been favored among the elders."

"But he couldn't be one if he married a human?" Calli asked.

Isa threw a look that clearly said she thought Calli an imbecile for even voicing the question. "Of course he couldn't. He ruined his chances when he took a human mate. If he had any children with Callista, his bloodline would be tainted." She shook her head. "Darrien told me he cared about me." For a moment, the harsh lines of years of hatred fell away and her lower lip trembled.

"He did love you, Isa," she said softly, "but he wasn't in love with you. Surely you realize that."

"You're wrong." Her voice turned hard as steel.

"He was confused. He didn't realize the mistake he made when he wedded Callista, and when she told him her news…" She inhaled deeply as if she were reliving a tragic day. "Callista was to have his young. I knew I had to take matters into my own hands. What kind of mongrel would have been born from such a union? We're shifters, and the child would have been mixed with human blood."

"But you have a human side," she said, though it seemed Isa had conveniently forgotten the fact."

"We are not human!" Her eyes flared gold.

Definitely a sore spot with her so Calli switched the conversation. "Even if you believed you were doing the right thing by eliminating Callista, you do realize by killing her you damned Darrien in more ways than one. He has lived centuries with his essence split, leaving him restless and never truly content. That's one hell of a way to show how much you love him. You've condemned him for eternity."

Her lips curved, but the smile didn't reach her eyes. "You knew the whole story, didn't you? Did you want me to confess? I have nothing to hide. I killed Callista and the brat she carried. There, I said it. I'm not sorry. I had every right."

Anger welled up inside of Calli and if her hands were free, she'd go after Isa for the travesty she caused in the name of love. Isa murdered a pregnant woman, and she left Darrien to pay for the sins she'd committed.

Isa tilted her head and pursed her lips. "You hate me."

Her statement hit home, surprising Calli. The emotion felt personal and long earned.

146

"Interesting, don't you agree?" Isa said. "Your soul recognizes me even if you don't truly grasp it." Then she chuckled, but Calli could find no reason why she'd find this humorous. "You question my affections for Darrien, don't you? You believe my methods were too severe." Isa's eyes glowed as if fire burned behind the irises, yet Calli wouldn't stop from voicing her opinion.

"If you loved Darrien, why didn't you prevent him from being sentenced? If you had stepped forward and said something in his defense, he wouldn't have been cursed."

She harrumphed again. "Did you expect me to confess I was the one who murdered his wife? I loved Darrien, but I'm not stupid."

Maybe not stupid, but crazy was up for debate. She bit the inside of her cheek to stop herself from saying as much. Anyway, it didn't seem as if Isa wanted a response from her.

"At the time," Isa said, "I didn't realize Spiro had the blessing from the goddess Hecate and was a powerful Necromancer. I knew he would mourn his daughter, but I miscalculated the depth of his sorrow."

Calli's mouth flattened into a hard line, and her brows rose. "You murdered his daughter, and you didn't expect him to be upset?" She couldn't believe the woman's rationale.

"Spiro's tribe also believed in reincarnation as the gryphon tribes did. His daughter would live again someday, but Spiro seemed to have forgotten in his grief. I had it all worked out, you see. I also knew by the time Callista's soul was reborn and she grew to adulthood, Darrien would no longer care." She waved her hand in dismissal.

That was where Isa was wrong. Darrien still pined for his wife. She saw it in the way he gazed at her. Even though Callista's memories were lost to her, the vision she experienced showed her a glimpse of what the two had shared. They had been in love and this woman had destroyed their lives. "What did you expect?" she asked Isa. "That you and Darrien would just fly off into the sunset and live happily-ever-after?"

Isa didn't answer, and the silence spoke more than words.

"My God, you did," she said in disbelief.

"With Callista out of the way, it was possible, but Spiro called his daughter back from the veil."

A small frown slipped across Calli's face. "What do you mean?"

"Spiro could summon souls," Isa said, "and he summoned his daughter to find out who'd been responsible for ending her life."

It didn't take a genius to know how that conversation turned out. "He would have the truth so why did he curse Darrien?" Calli asked. "He had nothing to do with the murder."

"Spiro still blamed Darrien for not realizing the threat and stopping me. So he cursed Darrien then went after all gryphons. He hunted them down and killed them one by one."

Pain settled behind Calli's heart as she realized what had happened because of Isa's treachery. "The tribe had nothing to do with what you did. Spiro punished all gryphons because of you?"

She lifted her shoulders in a shrug. "Spiro's grief turned to hatred, and he lashed out."

"And yet, you managed to survive." Calli couldn't

quite keep the terseness out of her voice."

"When I knew he was coming after the tribe, I took precautions."

"But what of the others? Why didn't you warn them?"

"I couldn't. I needed to buy some time so I could make my escape."

She was responsible for ending her species' lives, but she didn't seem upset. Maybe it was a survival instinct, or maybe she was just a cold-blooded woman who only cared about herself and her needs.

Isa sighed heavily. "Finally, Hecate became aware of Spiro's acts of revenge. He had misused his gifts from the goddess."

Took the goddess long enough to figure it out, Calli thought to herself, but she bit her tongue.

"Hecate stripped Spiro of his powers and forged it into a stone. It was then cast into the desert and never seen again until a student discovered it at a dig site. However, before I could retrieve it, the Guards of Judgment, who preside over all preternatural beings with their rules and regulations, confiscated it and from there you know where it ended up."

She'd have to find out more about this preternatural society, but for now she'd stick with this story. "It ended up at The Museum of Cursed Antiquities," Calli recapped. "So you hired me to steal the stone for you."

"Of course," she said with impatience.

"And you couldn't just waltz in there and take it because the museum is warded against preternatural beings."

For a moment Isa's composure slipped, but then

she must have decided it didn't matter if she spoke the truth. "Well, clever girl, I would have sent my men," she glanced at Bert, "but you saw how they botched the plan to extract you. I couldn't chance it, but I didn't expect you to fall for the beastie's charms. I'd swear you fell in love with Darrien all over again." Isa didn't appear thrilled with the prospect.

The claim weaved an unsettling path through Calli too. Was she in love with Darrien? Was it that easy to fall in love with someone if the stars were aligned just right, as Isa claimed? Didn't you have to date a person, get to know them, kiss…make love…well, all in good time. Love at first sight was for fairy tales, wasn't it? A dating service would just love to have a corner market on charting the stars and locating destined soul mates. She could see it now. Soul Mates Are Us, Dating Service.

"Your plan to have me steal the stone was nicely thought out," Calli said, "but if you think you're going to have your happy ending, you might want to rethink your plans again." She shifted her weight and flexed her hands for what little good it did. She was starting to lose feeling in her fingers and her shoulders ached, but her minor discomfort was nothing she couldn't endure. Her thoughts turned toward Darrien, and she swallowed the lump in her throat. "Let me remind you. Darrien has been shot and is bleeding out as we take this sweet trip down memory lane."

Isa rolled her eyes with such flourish there was no doubt Calli's comment irritated her. "You worry for nothing. Unless my men destroyed the gryphon statue, which I can assure you wouldn't be an easy task, Darrien will heal as soon as the sun sets. I've seen it happen before." Isa shook her head and sighed heavily as if she couldn't understand why Calli worried over a little bullet wound.

A flood of relief hit her full force, and she closed her eyes as she realized how scared she'd actually been for him. He would be all right. She opened her eyes again and glanced out the window. A carpet of color painted the heavens as the sun rode low in the sky. The change would happen soon. Hold on, Darrien, and then she silently prayed what Isa claimed would be the truth.

Isa let out a chuckle and covered her mouth. "His human side will believe he dreamt the whole fiasco." Her gaze slid over Calli with amusement. "He might not remember he had a nice chat with you. The curse is not so kind with the human aspect, most likely he can't handle the magic. Makes him quite forgetful. I've spoken to him before, you know. Twenty or so years ago… What a bore he'd been. Weak and unable to see without his glasses, and his horrible British accent just added to how dull he truly was. I will be glad when that part of his essence is gone."

Isa believed Nerdy Darrien would cease to exist once the curse was lifted? The human part of Darrien's essence was still him, just without the intense beastie side. He was witty and charming, and he most definitely was not weak or dull.

"It all comes full circle," Isa broke through her reverie, drawing Calli's attention, though the woman's words were spoken as if she were talking to herself. "Centuries ago, the curse placed on Darrien was issued on what you humans now call Halloween, most fitting don't you agree? Darrien's soul hovers between life and death, and this time of the year is when the veil between those two worlds is the thinnest. I plan on calling Spiro's soul from the veil and demand he release Darrien from the curse. Your blood will be the catalyst to bring it to fruition. Spiro will not refuse an audience when the blood of his daughter has done the summoning."

"Once the curse is broken, what then?" Calli asked. "How can you still hold onto the belief Darrien will want to be with you? He didn't want you the first time around. And what about the other souls you'll be releasing from the other side in the process? Paradise won't look so pretty then, will it? Especially when the walking dead try to eat your face for a snack."

Isa lifted her shoulders in a shrug as if she didn't care about the consequences to opening the eternal floodgates. "I'll be able to control the undead. I'll have Hecate's Stone. The souls cannot cross the threshold unless I demand it."

"Right," she said with sarcasm. "All's cool. My bad." Isa thrived on control, and she'd bet the woman wouldn't just close the doors to the underworld once she had Spiro remove the curse.

"Darrien will be beholden to me." She harrumphed with annoyance as she narrowed her eyes on her. "I'm freeing Darrien from the curse," she stated and lifted her chin. "He'll owe me the devotion I deserve," she said and nodded as if her evil plan made perfect sense.

Calli lifted her brows. Isa caused the dilemma Darrien found himself in, but had somehow decided she was doing him a favor by reversing it. Isa's demented expectations of how this night would end astounded Calli. This woman, who claimed she loved Darrien, didn't know him at all. Calli had spent a day and a night with the man and the gryphon, and she knew without a doubt that Darrien wouldn't want 'hell on earth' just to save his hide.

If only he could stop Isa, but Calli had no way of knowing how fast he'd heal from a gunshot wound once the change took place. Would he be up to full strength and able to take on a gryphon bent on making all her wishes come true, and the rest of the world be damned?

Calli's throat ached with regret. She most likely wouldn't make it out of this alive even if Darrien miraculously found her. The chances were slim to none. The two different Darriens didn't share memories. The nighttime version would most likely believe she'd left town while he was frozen as a statue. He'd have no reason to hunt her down since she'd left Hecate's Stone behind, and by the time it all became clear, it would be too late. Isa would have already killed her, and history would repeat itself.

Dying would really suck big time, but her heart went out to Darrien. He was convinced she'd been his wife in a past life, and with her death tonight, he would believe he failed her again.

Chapter Seventeen

As Darrien sputtered to life rising in his gryphon state, the pain in his chest knock the wind from him. His scream, a piping sound descended into a high-pitched keen. He clawed at the offensive wound with his talons, expelling the bullet lodged there. Then he shifted to his human form and fell to his knees, but the magic of the shift was already doing its job, healing the damage the bullet had caused. Tissue mended and the hole knitted, leaving only a slight discoloration where the bullet had entered.

Still crouched with his muscles tense, ready for anything, he made a quick visual sweep of the museum. Like the toll of a bell, the lack of sound proved just as deafening.

His gave wavered over the destruction of the room. A gunfight of some sort must have taken place while he stood in his stone-like state. His fingers rubbed the scar on his chest, wondering how a stray bullet came so close to penetrating his heart. Most amazing, how had it affected him when he'd been in his cursed state, a statue and not flesh? Where had Calli been when this all took place? Closing his eyes, he breathed in deeply, hoping to pick up her delicate scent, but instead the metallic coppery smell of violence gagged him.

"Blood," he murmured. Lots of it. Not just from him removing the bullet from his chest. More had been spilled. He ignored the sick twist in his gut and rose to his full height. He spotted the trail of dry blood on the floor and his gaze riveted to the desk. He strode over to it, half expecting to find a body sprawled on the floor. Blood stained the chair and bloody palm prints were pressed on the desk.

His frown deepened as his gaze retraced his steps. There had been a distinct trail of blood leading to the desk, but there was no trail leaving it. So much blood, but where was the body?

He scanned the items laying out on display upon the desktop, and spotted Hecate's Stone Calli had stolen from the museum. Was it her blood then? Panic clawed at him, making him want to shift and hunt down whoever had dared to harm her, but he reined in the beast. He could not lose focus and he needed his human side to make sense of the chaos. Then he realized the bloody prints were large handprints, and not petite ones. It gave him hope the blood wasn't Calli's after all.

He spotted a post-it with his name scrawled on it and a blood-smeared message. "You must see the video Calli filmed and the one I have made. It is vitally important," he read the message out loud. It was signed with his name as if he wrote the damn thing. He grabbed the phone and ripped off the post-it, tossing it on the desk. He hadn't handled one of these contraptions until now, but it seemed his fingers knew what to do. If he wasn't in such a panic, he might have wondered more about his knowledge and the strange message addressed to him, but right now all he could think about was if Calli still lived.

The first video played, and he witnessed how he changed from the beastie to... "The gods above..." His voice choked in a hoarse whisper of disbelief. He hadn't known this was what happened to him when the curse turned him into stone. He believed his whole essence lay dormant, but his human side separated like a spirit, leaving for the underworld, but it didn't leave, did it? The ghostlike essence became solid…human. Bless Calli's ingenious nature for filming the whole event.

He had always felt some part of him was missing, but he couldn't put a finger on what, and now he understood the restlessness, the reason he had difficulty controlling the beast. His human side lay dormant at night. His soul sliced in two and not one.

Once the first video ended, he searched for the other video he apparently left for himself. He slid his thumb over the play button. A man appeared on the screen with his features, but he was not entirely like him. There were distinct differences. Dark rimmed glasses adorned his face, and his words were peppered with a British cadence. Darrien couldn't help but notice the blood smeared on this man's forehead and the cardigan and shirt he wore were also soaked with blood.

His hand unconsciously went to his shoulder. Though the wound healed, he felt the ache where the bullet had been lodged.

"If you're playing this video," his daytime self said, "we have survived. I say we because I am you, or rather I'm the version allowed to walk in the sun while you sleep, and you're the version to walk the night—Bollocks," he cursed. "I believe you know what I mean." The video shifted abruptly, making him dizzy as it swung past the items in the museum before it finally focused on the gryphon statue. Then it abruptly shifted back to his human counterpart. "As you can see, we've been injured. The people who hired Calli came after her. The thug must have believed he left me for dead, but we are a stubborn lot. Yeah?"

He harrumphed and seriously wondered how this version of himself hadn't found himself shot way before now just for prattling on and not getting to the point.

"They took Calli," his daytime self said.

"What?" he gripped the phone and shook it as if he could throttle the daytime self for being so stupid as to let such a thing happen to Calli.

"I know you can track where they took her. Hurry!" The video went black.

It was a lot to take in and he would go over every last detail later, but first he must save Calli. If they shot the pathetic excuse of his other half when pity should have been offered, then that meant Calli's life would be forfeited once they realized she didn't have Hecate's Stone. They would show no mercy.

His gaze landed on the item. He would use it as a bargaining tool to see her released. The beastie could track them down later and give them what they truly deserved. His hand snaked out, grabbing the stone.

Now he needed something of Calli's to track her. His eyesight leveled on the phone he still clutched. He raised it to his nose and inhaled. Nothing, but he tried again, inhaling slowly. There… His nostrils flared as it picked up her delicate scent, lingering beneath the more odorous smell of his blood. He would find her.

He hurried toward the front door and was at a full run by the time his feet hit the pavement. He shifted, the magic rippling through his veins as the beast broke free with a ferocious gryphon's cry. He catapulted into the air with his hind legs, while his wings spread to their full length to catch the wind currents. He flew above the museum and circled once before he picked up Calli's scent. Then he headed in the direction where he would find her.

Chapter Eighteen

Bert shoved Calli into the motel room and she stumbled forward, nearly falling, but she caught herself on the table. "You should really think about changing how you treat a lady," she grumbled.

"When I see one, I'll think about it," he sneered, and let out a chuckle.

She wanted to say more, but she must pick her battles carefully. Her hands weren't tied behind her back any longer. One win for her.

When they were about to leave Isa's office, she offered the suggestion, since dragging a woman through the carport with her hands tied behind her back might draw unwarranted attention. Isa agreed with little convincing, and why wouldn't she when she could easily shift to a gryphon and rip out her throat? Still she had a smidgen of hope that she'd think of a way out of this mess. With her hands free, she could at least guarantee she'd go down fighting.

Isa followed them inside the motel room and secured the door behind her. Her eyes flickered with different shades of brown and amber as she took in the meager surroundings with little interest before she concentrated on Calli once more.

Calli sensed the beast lurking beneath the surface of Isa's calm exterior, ready to break free if crossed. Her eyes glowed brighter and they didn't appear quite…human.

"Where is it?" Isa demanded.

Calli had her dagger hidden in the nightstand next to the bed, but she highly doubted she'd make it there with Bert stationed beside her, and a dagger would be useless against Isa, who guarded the door to freedom. Her chance for escape proved limited, but there was a window in the bathroom, she might be able to squeeze through. The two other thugs under Isa's command stood guard in the parking lot just outside the room. If she chose the window as her means of escape, she'd have to make a run for it on foot. She wondered how long it would take a gryphon to spot her from the air. Her guess? Not long.

So the plan had holes in it, but it was all she had right now. She still had time to figure out a better one. Isa wanted the stone, and she needed her alive for the ritual. She could bide some time without it costing her too dearly—like having her head severed from her body.

Her gaze shifted to Bert who eyed her as if he hoped she'd try something so he could step in. They needed her alive, she reminded herself. Alive being the key word, but not necessarily unharmed as Bert had mentioned earlier.

She stood tall and folded her arms across her chest and prayed a good plan would pop into her head and soon. "I don't have the stone," she finally voiced.

Isa's eyes glowed brighter, the only indication she was losing her cool. "What do you mean you don't have the stone? Why did you have us bring you back to your motel, if not to retrieve it?"

She lifted a shoulder. "I believe the statement speaks for itself."

"Where is it?" Isa demanded as if her freaky eyes and authoritative voice would make her give up the location.

Calli leaned against the table as a new plan started to take fruit. It wasn't the best plan in the world, but it was probably a smidgen better than the bathroom escape. "It's at the museum," she said smugly. Telling the truth was really the best policy. As long as the stone stayed there, Isa couldn't get to it. However, her goons were another story. By now Darrien would be the gryphon. They would have to get past him, and she had a very good hunch they wouldn't last the evening with a testy gryphon shifter.

Isa let out a screech sounding like an eagle, only louder and more menacing. Even she could tell Isa was losing control and fought to keep the beast contained.

She pushed away from the table. If Isa shifted in the room, it wouldn't end well. The wingspread of the beast would do considerable damage. Heads would roll... and she didn't want it to be hers. Calli was about to say something, anything that may keep Isa from exploding into full gryphon mode, but before she could utter a word, the door to the room crashed opened, leaving it swinging on its hinges.

Darrien stood in the archway wearing his jeans and an *I love Rock and Roll* T-shirt, but he still managed to appear like a Greek god bent on wreaking havoc. Somehow, he'd been able to track her. Somehow, he knew she needed him too. Damn, that was really hot. A wise woman knew when it was in her best interest to have a man sweep in and save the day. This was it, and her heart did a flip-flop.

"You will let her go," Darrien's voice boomed, and

his eyes glimmered with gold light.

Bert made a move, his hand going for the knife strapped to his belt, but Darrien caught sight of his attempt and leveled his gaze in the man's direction.

"I wouldn't advise you to come any closer," Darrien threatened and lifted his hand, shifting just enough to reveal his razor-sharp talons. Bert's weapon looked like a butter knife when compared to a gryphon's claw.

Bert's face paled and he glanced at Isa for guidance. If the thugs outside hadn't stopped Darrien, it was pretty safe to say, Bert wouldn't have a chance against him either.

Isa lifted her hand and gave Bert a slight shake of her head. Bert backed away, but she could tell he still itched for a fight.

Calli's lips curved. *You tell them what's what, Darrien.* She was glad to see he was whole and healthy just as Isa had predicted he would be, and he was just as bossy and demanding as she remembered. God, she loved that about him.

Darrien glanced her way and gave her a slight nod of reassurance before he turned his attention on Isa once more. "Calli is leaving with me," he told her with no room for negotiation. Any other person may have been intimidated to adhere to such a demand, but Isa wasn't any ordinary woman. She was like Darrien and could make demands of her own, but being off-hinged, the danger-meter went up another few notches.

Isa regained her composure as she turned to greet Darrien with a bird-like tilt of her head. "You still protect her. After all this time, a mere human woman. She doesn't even remember being with you."

Of course, she had to bring that up, but it seemed Darrien didn't care. "Isa," Darrien said and narrowed his eyes, "you have not changed in the least." His gaze swept over her with renewed interest as if sizing up a potential adversary. "Why do you do this? Have I not suffered enough from your treachery?"

"You have it all wrong." She approached him, gently placing a hand on his forearm. His gaze followed the action, and he did nothing to stop her. Only the tick at his jaw revealed he did not like her hand on him. "I am here to free you from your curse," she told him. "We can be together then. We could be happy. It's all I ever wanted for us."

"You are why I was cursed in the first place. Did you think I would forget what you did?" Then his eyes again turned bright gold and all other shades were absorbed by the glow.

Isa let her hand slide away. "It was a mistake to kill Callista. I see that now." She nodded as if she just reasoned it all out. "I should have waited. You would have tired of her, as she grew old and withered. Humans do not age well, and she would have eventually perished and turned to dust."

"What you have always failed to understand is that I love her," Darrien said simply. "I love her for always. Young, old, turned to dust...for always."

Calli rolled her eyes. Grand pledges, but really, he shouldn't provoke the jealous gryphon with a grudge against humans, especially when said gryphon sought Darrien's affections. Calli glanced at Isa, wondering what she would do next now that Darrien pretty much told her to take a flying leap off the nearest mountain and nosedive to the ground. Yep, not a pretty sight.

"Well, then…" Isa inhaled deeply then let it out again with a sigh. "We shall see if your claim still holds true." Her gaze landed on Calli as she pointed her finger at her. "By the gods, I condemn you…" she began the curse in English then reverted to an ancient language, Calli didn't understand, but it was obvious Darrien did.

"No-o-o!" He lunged for Isa, but she waved her hand at him, and he flew against the wall, pinned like a bug on a corkboard. Obviously, Isa picked up a few tricks during the centuries and Darrien wasn't privy to them. "Run, Calli," Darrien ordered and she wasn't going to question him. Whatever Isa was reciting, it obviously wouldn't bode well for her.

She whirled around toward the bathroom. She guessed the 'escape out the window' plan was going to be it.

She'd only taken a few steps, but halted, not because she wanted to, but because her feet seemed to have stopped working. She couldn't move. Her limbs were frozen. Isa's chant was doing something to her. She could still hear Darrien demanding Isa to stop, but then her hearing dimmed, and her eyesight faded next. Panic welled inside of her, but she could do nothing, not even cry out for help.

Chapter Nineteen

"You will pay for this, Isa," Darrien cried, the threat seeming ridiculous since he was pinned to the wall and unable to reach her. Isa had turned his beloved to stone, and he knew the horrors of enduring such a fate.

Isa glanced his way and with a wave of her hand, she released him. He fell to the floor, landing in a crouched position. It took all his self-control not to lunge at the woman, but he couldn't kill her...not yet. She had to reverse the curse she'd placed on Calli. He refused to let her suffer such a fate. Dead, but not. Just frozen as time ticked by, forgotten and unloved. This was a fate worse than death, a torture no one should ever endure.

"What's wrong, my sweet? You didn't like my trick?" She flashed her hand his way. An intricate ring, still shimmering with magic, adorned her ring finger. "Picked up this lovely piece of jewelry from a wizard. I can turn anything to stone with a few said words. The silly man should have never allowed me to hold it." She let out a long and tired sigh. "He still stands guard in my personal collection, along with an angel, but that's another story." She uttered a deep throaty chuckle which made Darrien clench his fist so not to lash out. "Now your beloved can be at your side," she purred. "It's what you always wanted, right?" Isa arched one elegant brow. "Both of you can stand side by side in the

Museum of Cursed Antiquities for all eternity, a matching pair of idiots," she snarled the last word to bring home her point. As if he hadn't caught the sarcasm dripping from her speech.

He slowly stood to his full height. "Let her go and I'll do whatever you want," he said slowly and calmly as if he approached an animal ready to lunge. He'd vow to never see Calli again if it meant she would live.

Isa clapped her hands and chortled again. "How noble, but you see what I want is for her to be gone from our lives forever. I want Hecate's Stone, Darrien. I will use her blood, summon Spiro, and have him release you from the curse."

"And what will happen to Calli if I hand over the stone?"

"So you do have it. On you?" Her gaze slid over him as if she wondered where he'd hidden it on his person.

He didn't keep her guessing but withdrew the item she coveted from his pocket and held it between his forefinger and thumb for her to see. She reached for it, but he whipped it out of her range above his head. "Nay. You have not answered my question. What will happen to Calli?"

She lifted her elegant shoulders in a shrug. "She is dead already, if I do nothing," she told him. She glanced at the stone figure of Calli forever frozen in a position of her trying to flee. "At least with the ritual I intend to do, she'll be released from her prison and her soul will have the chance to be reborn once again."

"You are not endearing me to see your side of things," he seethed with anger. Damn the infernal female. He would kill her. He would rip her to shreds

166

and scatter her body in the four regions. "You do not need to drain her for the ritual to work," he said and was surprised his voice remained steady.

"Perhaps not, but it would be much more fun to see her bleed out...again."

He inwardly flinched at her words, the dig driving deeper into his heart, where the wound had never quite healed. Isa had watched Callista die, had waited until she drew her last breath.

"You never did see things my way," she pouted then her eyes turned cold. "Let me speak plainly. You don't have a choice." She glanced at Bert.

The man hadn't so much as shied away from what transpired here tonight. He must have been with Isa a long time or perhaps he shared in her diabolical tendencies and saw nothing amiss.

"Bring the statue outside," she ordered Bert. "And be careful not to drop it," she added before she sauntered by Darrien, then paused in the doorway. "We don't want Calli to lose a limb...or her pretty little head. It would be such a shame if that happened." Her lips curved into a smile and her eyes shimmered with maniacal delight. She enjoyed inflicting pain. Be it physical or not. No matter what he did or promised, she would not let Calli live.

He recalled Isa as a child, when she was wild and carefree. He remembered how she would often times tag along with him and his friends when they flew to the mountaintop where they could look over the lands, the village, and the sea beyond.

She was a few years younger, but she never slowed them down. She could keep up with most of the males. Fast and sure, diving toward the water then soaring as if she could reach the heavens. Then her laughter of pure joy would make him smile.

He'd known she was fond of him. He'd seen the sly glances when she thought he wouldn't notice, but he truly believed it to be a fanciful attraction of youth. He thought she'd grow to realize they were never meant to be.

From the moment he met Callista he knew she would be his, and she shared the same belief. The attraction between them could not be ignored. Her mere laughter brought joy to his heart. She was as sweet as she was clever. He sighed wearily.

In truth, he had forgotten about Isa by the time she was old enough to find a mate and start a family. If only he had talked to her, convinced her she would find someone else who would love her with all his heart. If only…

He could go on forever with a list of what he could have done, but it proved too late for any of it. Isa was no longer a young female, tagging along to see what mischief she would find. She'd forgotten how to enjoy life. Hatred governed her, and she took happiness away from others as if consuming their glee would somehow fill the emptiness in her heart.

Darrien followed Isa. She paused when she spotted her two men who had been stationed outside the motel room. "Are they dead?" she asked Darrien.

"No," he told her. He had no need to kill them. He caught them unaware and knocked them out with little effort.

Her shoulders lifted in a shrug. "Useless, those two. I wish you would have saved me the trouble." She continued on her way without a backward glance. Her steps were sure and proud, and her hips swayed back and forth with confidence. She had the walk of a warrior back from battle and carting the riches for the coffers.

She did not realize he had not given up, not in the least, but with Calli frozen, he had no choice but to play along for the moment. Isa had pushed him into a corner, but this time he would not allow her to take the woman he loved from this world. By the gods, once he had vowed to protect Callista and failed. This was his chance to make good on his promise by saving Calli tonight.

Isa halted her steps in the center of the parking lot. Bert placed the statue of Calli down and stood guard as if he too had turned to stone with the way he folded his arms across his chest and waited for further instructions.

Darrien regarded Isa curiously, wondering what she planned next.

"Hand over Hecate's Stone, if you will," Isa demanded of him. She outstretched her hand, palm up as if he would just plop the item into her clutches and call it a day.

She would be sadly disappointed. "Undo the magic you cast on Calli," he countered. "I will have my proper goodbye before you perform any ritual. You owe me that much." He took the steps separating him from Calli and stood in front of her, afraid to touch her and feel the cold stone and not the heat of her flesh. "Hecate's Stone for Calli's release," he said, just to make sure she understood the terms.

Isa's eyes narrowed becoming dark slits of fury. "What makes you believe you have the upper hand and

can make demands? I'm in control of the situation."
She tapped her chest with her index finger. "I've turned
your little twit to stone, and you're cursed, a slave to
the hours of the day. I don't see how this gives you an
advantage to demand anything."

He gave her a slow appraising look. Not a hair out
of place, and her outfit gave her the polished,
sophisticated appearance of a woman who could
command an empire, but the slight trembling of her
lower lip gave her away. She never could command if
she could not control her own emotions. Isa only looked
after herself, and when she didn't get her way she
pouted and stomped her feet.

A memory of her as a child came to mind. She'd
wanted a trinket her brother had brought back from a
raid, but he wanted to give it to a girl he sought to
court. Isa had destroyed the trinket in a fit of rage then
took to the sky, screeching until the tribe thought their
ears would bleed. There were other temper tantrums
through the years, but no one foresaw the treachery
she'd be capable of exacting. She'd murdered his wife,
caused the destruction of their tribe, and the gods only
knew what other immoral acts she'd done through the
centuries. She'd mentioned a wizard and his ring. No
doubt others had suffered at her hands. By all the stars
in the heavens, she had skirted justice long enough, but
first he must play her game for just a little while longer,
before he changed the rules and finished this for good.

"I have lived with my losses," he told her with a
shrug as if he didn't care if the curse lasted another
century or not. "So be it," he said. "Being cursed will
be just another day. You threaten me with nothing, Isa.
I will have my goodbye with Calli, and you will set her

free. It's my condition if you want me to stand by your side," he told her.

She seemed to consider his words as her keen eyes bore into him. She most likely wondered if he would deceive her, but in the end, she chose what she wanted to believe. She wanted him, yes, but as a person who wants an object to display on a mantle, a prize she'd won.

Isa turned toward Calli with hands raised. The wind picked up, swirling around them as words from the old world flew from her lips, and like a performer enjoying the tune, Isa belted them out as sweet and sure as an opera singer on a stage.

He took a step back, allowing the magic to take hold of Calli. Then slowly, he witnessed her awaking from the curse. Her skin lightened to a healthy glow as the stone turned to flesh. Her moss-colored eyes flashed with life, and she drew in a ragged breath.

Inside the motel, she'd been fleeing the scene, and it was as if time had stood still for her. With the curse lifted, her momentum continued. Her flight abruptly resumed. Her feet sprinted forward as her last movement set the pace.

He'd anticipated this would happen and braced himself as she slammed into him. His arms came around her so she wouldn't fall. "You are safe," he told her and closed his eyes, placing a kiss on top of her head. For centuries, he had wrestled with the guilt of what happened the day Isa had killed his wife. He'd been too late to save his sweet Callista, but he wouldn't fail Calli. Of this, he vowed.

Calli's body relaxed into his embrace, and she just breathed. What a wonderful sound it was to hear the intake of breath and the whoosh as it was being released once more. Her heartbeat reached his ears, a thump-thump, thump-thump, a little fast, but steady. She leaned back and lifted her chin to meet his eyes.

"What…happened?" she asked, her voice raspy as she cleared her throat. Her brow furrowed with unease.

All he wanted to do was smooth those lines of stress and tell her everything would be all right. Instead, he leaned down and kissed her, silencing her questions with the caress. She didn't push him away but wrapped her arms around him. He inhaled the scent of her and the memory of holding his wife in this same fashion came back to him full force, but he also knew this was Calli, a thief who had awakened his desire to live. He didn't want to break the connection, but he must if he were to finish what Isa had started so long ago. He cradled Calli's head as he whispered in her ear, "Trust me."

He let the magic roll over him, and he shifted into the gryphon with Calli cradled in his claws. Her startled intake of breath at the sudden change of embrace couldn't be helped. Thankfully, she didn't struggle to be free from him, but quickly settled and held on. Such a brave and trusting woman and his heart swelled with his love for her.

His wings spread wide, and the wind fluttered over his feathers with encouragement. He pushed off, his back paws giving him the leverage he needed to take flight.

Isa screeched the sounds of her betrayal before switching to the language of gryphons to blast him further. It had been so long since he heard his language spoken by another, he wished it hadn't been used for curses and in anger. He glanced down below where Isa stood with Bert at her side. He noticed the other two men he'd knocked out earlier were jogging toward Isa. She appeared to be issuing orders, her hands flying as she spoke. Then she glanced skyward. Even from this distance, he could see fury in her eyes as bright as the blazing sun. A second later, the shimmer of energy surrounded her as she shifted into her gryphon form to pursue him.

That was his cue to go. His long wingspan gave him the advantage and his head start even more. He kept well ahead of Isa, but he knew she would figure out where he headed soon enough.

Chapter Twenty

Calli's mind still felt scrambled from her ordeal, but she managed to hang onto Darrien as he flew high above the world below. Her teeth chattered, but she didn't think it was because of the cold. Trauma, shock, the fact she was clutched in a gryphon's claws…heck, all of the above could be the cause.

She closed her eyes and let the wind blow through her hair. A scent surrounded her, a blend of sand, spice, and male heat. A strange combination, but she knew it to be Darrien, who had morphed into a gryphon. The steady flap of his wings lulled her too. She was safe. He would keep her safe. The whisper of unease, teasing her senses, flitted away on the wind and she relaxed, knowing he wouldn't let anything happen to her if he could help it.

Darrien had told her how much Callista had loved to fly with him. Now, she understood why. Despite the life and death situation they were in, the thrill of soaring through the air was exhilarating.

Her gaze took in the scene below and wondered where Darrien was heading. They'd left the motel far behind, and the desert below proved a featureless black ocean with only a few pinpricks of stars and a wan, sickle moon to light the path, but then she spotted a building in the distance. Maybe they were heading for the museum. As if Darrien sensed her thoughts, he veered to the left toward the building, the course proving she'd been right.

Fast and sure, Darrien's wings took them closer until he was above the museum. He circled around the parking lot, then lower and lower until he hovered near the ground. She anticipated he was going to release her and scooted forward. The drop hadn't been far, but her limbs weren't fully recovered from her ordeal. She stumbled, and fell to her knees, but Darrien was there beside her in seconds. He had shifted to his human side and reached for her, helping her to her feet.

"Are you well?" he asked with concern.

"Just peachy keen." Her father used to use those words when he was far from all right. It was his standard line after he had chemo. He claimed if he said he was peachy keen enough times eventually his body would catch up to what his brain wanted to be true.

"Does that mean you are ill? Your pallor has turned a ghastly shade not conclusive with health."

She might have laughed, but she just didn't have it in her. Instead, she gave him a huge smile. "I'm working on fine. Can you give me a moment?" Her mouth felt like she swallowed sand and she licked her lips, hoping to find moisture.

"You need water," he told her.

Before she could respond, he flitted away then returned before she could lick her lips again. He held out a water bottle with one hand, the lid already removed, while his other hand rested at her elbow to keep her steady. She fisted her hands then opened them again with hopes the tingly feeling at her fingertips would cease to plague her. Her circulation had been hampered big time. She reached for the bottle and managed not to drop it as she took a generous drink.

The cool liquid soothed her parched throat and worked like an elixir. A surge of energy raced through her veins after each sip she took.

As she indulged, she considered what happened. Isa had been stronger than she imagined, more powerful and dangerous. The woman was a gryphon, but she also had a few lethal tricks, and Calli couldn't say she looked forward to an encore. She remembered there had been a wizard and an angel in her office. Made her wonder if they had fallen victim to Isa's wrath and she turned them to stone. It would account for why she thought the statues had seemed creepy in some way, not quite right. Maybe she had sensed their souls trapped inside the marble.

"I am sorry." Darrien said.

"You're sorry? You have nothing to be sorry about. That witch with a capital B is the one who will be sorry. She turned me to stone!" She ran a hand over her face and inhaled deeply. Glad she could manage such a simple act as breathing.

"She will pay for what she has done—past and present offences. You mark my words." His eyes shifted to the eagle-like blink before returning to his more human look. His eyes were unusual no matter what, but when they glowed and the irises turned a different shape, it brought home the fact he was not entirely human.

He still held onto her elbow. Probably because he feared she would tumble to the ground, but she could feel her toes again, and her energy had returned to full strength. Water truly did replenish. She vowed from this day forward, she'd keep extra water bottles on hand.

Darrien shifted his position so he stood in front of her. His fingers smoothed her hair from her face and his gaze held such longing it made her legs feel like wet noodles all over again. She gripped his forearms to keep her balance without falling. In truth, she was already falling—in love, that is—with this wonderfully honorable shifter.

"You truly are beautiful, all windblown and determined," he told her. "You are so very brave, Calli Angelis. I blessed the stars the moment you walked into my museum to commit thievery."

Her lips twitched into a smile. "You do know how to dazzle a girl with sweet talk."

He looked confused, but then he chuckled. "I have not wooed a woman in a long time."

She sighed. "Funny thing is, I kind of like how you're wooing."

"Brave, beautiful, and most forgiving..." He cupped her face and leaned down to press his lips to hers.

They were moments away from Isa's wrath, yet she couldn't help but take what Darrien offered. Who knew if they would ever get another chance? If Isa had her way, she and Darrien would be bookends in her office, or maybe she'd put them next to the wizard and the angel statue.

As his kiss demanded more of her attention, the near emptied water bottle slipped from her fingers so she could hold onto Darrien. He tasted dark and dangerous—everything she needed right now. She closed her eyes and savored his exquisite caress. He half growled, half chuckled as he pulled her closer. His calloused hands were rough on her cheek, but she didn't mind. The intensity and the immediacy of the attraction she felt for him mystified her, and yet with stolen moments like this, she felt she'd finally come home.

He ended the kiss sooner than she would have liked, and when he pulled away, she teetered forward as if he were her lifeline to the oxygen she needed. Her skin felt warm and tingly. It could be the effects of being turned to stone or it could be Darrien's kisses playing havoc with her libido. She had a hunch it was the latter.

"Isa will be upon us in a moment," he warned her. "She will pick up my scent soon enough. Please go inside the museum. You shall be safe there."

She'd been turned to stone and her limbs hadn't fully recovered, leaving her feeling as if she wore lead-lined boots and weights on her wrists, but she wasn't going to hide in the museum and leave him out here to face Isa.

"Are you all right?" Tender concern laced his words, and she realized she hadn't said anything about his request. He shifted his gaze skyward as if he expected Isa to dive down and attack. She still might.

"You'll be safe inside the museum too." Her hand snaked out and tugged on his sleeve. His gaze riveted to her. "She can't enter the building," she said. "It's warded against preternatural creatures—at least ones that aren't cursed," she corrected her claim. "You can easily hold off her men from inside if they decide to join her."

"I will not hide." He straightened his back and stood taller. "I must end this once and for all. Isa will not stop until she has her way. She does not care who she must harm to achieve the goal. We have but one

178

chance." He pulled out Hecate's Stone from the pouch attached at his belt. He was about to hand it to her so she could put in a safe place in the museum, but the stone started to glow and throb with energy. No longer did it appear black, but all shades of the rainbow pulsed inside of it, the color changing with each pulse. The air around them became thicker and a wind picked up ruffling their hair as if the stone commanded it.

"What's it doing?" she shouted. Each pulse of the stone increased the momentum of the wind, and dust blew from the desert floor, making it difficult to breathe.

"I don't know," he shouted back as the stone burst with energy like a bolt of lightning streaking across the sky.

An area large and oval took shape a few feet in front of them. The area rippled like water, reminding her of rocks skipping across a lake. When it smoothed, they viewed another world, though the parking lot remained all around it on either side. It was like looking through a portal on a ship, but much larger, generous enough for Darrien to step through without hunching down.

In the other world, blue, purple, and gold colored the heavens as if the sun had just set and all the colors bled into the horizon where the land met the sky. A river dark and foreboding reached the portal's edge but didn't flow over into their world. Instead, the water teased by rising and falling as it attempted to cross, but a barrier of some sort held it at bay.

"The veil between the worlds has been revealed to us," Darrien said, his voice thick with emotion.

179

Chapter Twenty-One

Darrien glanced at the stone glowing, pulsing with energy, and knew it had somehow triggered the doorway to the Otherworld to reveal itself. The veil was at its thinnest on Halloween, the day the humans celebrated with parties and costumes. They'd forgotten when the veil thinned, they could communicate with the dead.

Hecate's Stone amplified where the boundaries rested, making the Otherworld visible to anyone who might happen by, be they mortal or not. They didn't have to believe to see it. The portal stood, both beautiful and frightening, for all to view.

He turned to Calli and shouted to be heard over the roaring wind. "There was blood on the stone when I found it on the desk in the museum. Whose was it?" he asked, but he had a hunch he already knew.

She shouted back, her words coming to him as if she stood on a precipice high above him, her voice strained and faraway. "It has to be your blood... from your human side. I gave the stone to you for safekeeping, but one of Isa's men shot you."

"My alter ego left me such a message on your mobile," he grumbled and rubbed his chest, though the bullet wound had healed completely now.

"He did?" she asked, appearing surprised, and he realized she would be. She'd already been kidnapped and hadn't known his other half's outcome.

He nodded. "An interesting conversation, I must say. It is how I knew you were in trouble." He glanced at the portal where the river appeared dark and foreboding. He could see movement beneath the surface—arms outstretched, and faces contorted as if in pain. The souls of the lost, he imagined with a shudder.

"You can command the dead, can't you?" She too stared at the portal with meaning. "You can control what's happening right now. Your blood has activated the doorway to open. You can request an audience with Spiro. Surely, he can't still hold a grudge against you. It's been centuries."

The last memory of Spiro had been when he'd been chained in the cellar and awaited sentencing. Spiro tortured him further with his plans to kill his tribe, and even promised not to spare the children. No amount of begging could convince Spiro to go after the one responsible. Isa had acted alone, but by then Spiro's grief had festered into hatred, and there was no reasoning with the man. Spiro had cursed him and had gone after his tribe without mercy. The man's hatred ran deep, and he could not be sure it didn't follow him into the afterlife.

It wasn't until decades later, and by a mere chance, he learned what had happened once Spiro gave the order to annihilate his tribe. A thief had entered the museum when it still had been stationed in Greece. The man knew of the gryphon tribe which once lived on the isle of Andros, but no longer existed. He'd been devastated by the news, and yet he had not been surprised. He'd sensed the loss of the tribe, felt it in his heart, then thief had confirmed it. For that valuable information, he'd allowed the thief to walk away unharmed.

Calli placed a hand on his arm. "You must try," she said as if sensing his lack of confidence.

He brushed a tendril of hair away from her face, but it fell over one eye again as if the wind would not allow the gesture.

She was right. He had to at least make an attempt to reason with Spiro, and if he would not hear his plea, or if the price proved too high, he would close the veil and so be it.

Conjuring and opening a portal always came with a price. Before leaving the museum tonight, he pocketed a few ancient coins from the bottom drawer of the desk as his daytime self, suggested he do in his video. The ferryman would demand payment for carting a soul back and forth. His hand slipped into his front pocket of his jeans and fingered the etched coins for reassurance he still had them. He hoped the coins would suffice.

He turned to tell Calli of his plans, but he caught sight of a shadow overhead, fast and true as it darted across the heavens. Isa had found them.

She landed with grace and shifted to her human form as soon as her paws hit the ground. Her gaze wasn't focused on them but transfixed on the portal between the worlds. Since her arrival, the river of souls beckoned and keened, somehow louder and more desperate to be heard.

"What are you waiting for?" Isa turned to peer at him. "Summon Spiro and request he reverse the curse," she ordered. "You hold the power in your hands, Darrien. The ferryman must obey you." Isa's eyes were golden in color and more bird-like, and her hands had shifted to talons as if her human side proved difficult to hold.

Gryphons lived long lives, but they were not immortal. Yet Isa had lived centuries longer than any gryphon in the history of his tribe. Of course, he was excluded. The curse was to blame for his long existence. "How do you still live, Isa?" he asked with a tilt of his head. Confusion lit her features before she realized why he would ask such a question.

Her talons retracted and her slender hands appeared as she smoothed back her hair in a desperate attempt to keep it out of her eyes, but the wind fought her attempts. "There are ways. Magic can be bought and so can immortality."

"And did these individuals you brokered a deal with live to tell the tale?" He knew what happened to the wizard who once owned a certain ring on her finger.

Isa pursed her lips, and her silence gave him the answer. She stole, most likely murdered, and took what she wanted. She didn't look back or feel remorse. "I did it for you," she said as if she read his mind and knew he judged her for the immoral acts she'd committed.

His brows rose, not because he was surprised at her admission, but because he could not believe she had the audacity to claim she did her evil deeds in his name. Isa's obsession for him ruled her thoughts and actions, and in the process, she'd forgotten what it meant to truly love someone. Her heart had hardened as if it were made of stone.

"Summoning Charon comes with a price, Isa," he said. Charon ferried the souls to the underworld, and he would not like to be ordered around. Of this, he was certain.

Isa glanced at Calli briefly with a nod. "She is pure

of heart. She will not suffer. Save yourself, Darrien. It's your only chance to be free. Take it. Offer her to Charon as payment. He will gladly take a good soul."

Before he could comment, the sounds of tires screeching as they skidded to a halt could be heard over the howling wind. Isa's men had arrived by car. No doubt, they'd seen the light Hecate's Stone had produced.

He dare not take his eyes off Isa as the doors of the car slammed shut. The unmistakable crunching of boots on gravel reached his ears next, indicating they were running toward them.

Isa kept her eyes on him also, but she held up her hand in a wave of warning for her men to stand down. "Well? What are you going to do?" she asked.

He wanted to laugh at her. Truly, she didn't believe he'd sacrifice Calli for his freedom, but Isa's eyes brightened with triumph. She thought he would do it. After all, it would be what she would do. What she had planned to do, if the stone rested in her palm.

Darrien shook his head sadly and turned away from Isa. His gaze found Calli, who stood straight and proud. No fear marred her expression, and for a split second, he saw his Callista's eyes gazing back at him. He swallowed the lump in his throat and blinked. Calli stood there once more.

He mouthed, "Trust me," and hoped she would. She gave him a slight nod of understanding. He turned away from her then and stepped forward with the stone gripped in his hand as he held it in front of him. "I call upon Charon to deliver the soul of Spiro to the doors between worlds. I have the stone with the power of the goddess Hecate, her essence is in the palm of my hand,

and my blood summons thee."

When nothing happened, he tried again, using ancient words spoken first in Greek then in Latin. *"Ego sum te peto et videre queto."* He'd chant the summons in every language until it worked. "I seek you and demand to see you." The howling wind increased around them, but the weather beyond the doorway remained tranquil. Then in the distance, he spotted a long boat made of fine wood and etched with symbols. Possibly wards to keep the newly dead from escaping once they stepped into the boat... Or perhaps, they were to prevent the damned in the river from capsizing the craft. Whichever the case, the symbols glowed with magic.

Two figures stood inside the boat, one holding a pole and guiding it toward the portal's entrance, and the other stood with his hands clasped as if in prayer.

"It is Charon," Isa breathed and her lips curved. "He brings Spiro with him. Do you not see, Darrien?"

Darrien could understand her reverence toward Charon. One did not have an audience with the ferryman unless he came to ferry your soul to the underworld. His gaze shifted to Spiro who was garbed in dark tattered robes that were worn in places, nothing like he would have donned in life. Darrien couldn't help but wonder if the clothing depicted his placement in the underworld. Not favored, he would imagine.

Charon frowned, his lips thin as they pursed together, indicating his displeasure at being summoned, and more so when he realized Darrien held a stone with powers meant for a necromancer. Obviously, the ferryman didn't look kindly on death charmers. They would make his life difficult if they summoned the dead back to the living—even if it were for only a few minutes. It would make Charon's job that much more troublesome.

Once the boat reached the door's edge, Charon tethered the boat to a pillar to keep the craft in place for this impromptu meeting. "Who summons the soul of Spiro?" Charon asked. The burdens of his duties of centuries past were deeply etched into his weathered skin. His robes of gray swirled around him in the gentle wind on his side of the realm, teasing both his hair and long beard. He may ask who summoned him, but the request proved a formality, since his gaze bore into Darrien.

"I do, ferryman." He bowed in respect to the ancient being.

"Step forward then, but do not cross the threshold, Darrien of the gryphon tribe of Andros," he warned. "Your soul teeters between life and death, and I cannot guarantee the souls of the underworld will not claim you as one of their own out of spite."

He stared at the river where the wrathful were punished, being drowned in the muddy waters for all eternity. Their skin was drained of color, gray and lifeless, but they withered and moaned as they fought among themselves. He shivered at the thought of joining their fate.

He turned to Calli. Her green eyes were huge with fatigue, and he realized how this night had taken its toll on her. Yet, her strength washed over to him, and he offered her his hand. He wanted her at his side and away from Isa. Calli's hand felt so small and delicate in his. He raised her hand to his lips, and he brushed a kiss across her knuckles before they both took a few cautious steps closer to the portal, making sure to keep their feet planted in the realm of the living.

Standing this close to the doorway, the wind ceased to plague them, as if they'd stepped into the eye of the storm, where the world appeared calm, but their presence seemed to aggravate the souls. Their filmy, bluish-colored eyes, glazed with death, followed their every move. Their moans and outstretched hands a plead for help, only the damned found no comfort ever.

A movement in his peripheral vision told him Isa had joined them, but he remained focused on Spiro. The man's gaze blazed a trail from Darrien's face to his snakeskin boots then back up. His contempt blasted through him with his scorn, despite the threshold separating them. It appeared even in death his hatred hadn't lessened. It had thrived.

"If you wish to speak to me about the curse, you waste your time, Darrien," Spiro said. "I have no wish to speak to you. When Hecate confronted me, I chose death over releasing your soul. I suffer for my sins, but I rejoice knowing you have suffered more."

Darrien didn't blame Spiro for lashing out at him. The man had trusted him with his beloved daughter, a treasure he could never replace, and Darrien felt the loss just as deeply. He blamed himself for her death as much as Isa was at fault. He should have recognized Isa's jealousy and stopped her, but he'd been so in love he missed the warning signs. "I have accepted my fate gladly, Spiro," he told him and meant it.

Calli's presence gave him strength to face Spiro, but he had to do this next part alone. He gave her hand a quick squeeze before he let her go. He then chanced another step closer to the portal.

187

His admission and acceptance of the punishment Spiro dealt him seemed to surprise the man, and he lost some of his haughtiness. He pursed his lips as if he fought to remain steadfast in his oath not to hear him out, but in the end his curiosity prompted him to change his mind. "Go on then," Spiro demanded. "Say what you must so I may return to the land of the dead." He folded his arms across his chest.

"To the point, then. I bring to you the one responsible for Callista's death," Darrien announced.

"What are you doing?" Isa's gaze riveted to him, and her voice hitched in alarm. She took a step back as if to flee, but he was quicker and grabbed her upper arm. "Unhand me." She struggled to be free, but he would not allow her to escape. When her thugs moved forward to help, he warned them away with a quick look, his eyes blazing like fire. "Come closer and you'll suffer her fate as well."

Bert glanced at the door to the underworld with the black river and the souls crying out for help, and he made the decision for himself and his comrades. "Let's go. We didn't sign up for this." They backed away before turning on their heels at a full run to put as much distance between them and the archway as possible.

"Come back, you fools," Isa called after them, but a second later, he heard the slam of car doors and the screeching of tires. Her men had abandoned her. So much for loyalty.

Spiro's nostrils flared as he leveled his gaze on Isa. "How did you avoid my wrath?" he asked her. "You murdered my daughter, and I sent my hoplites armed with weapons. They were to destroy all your kind? How is it you still stand in the land of the living?"

"You wronged my tribe and me as well." Isa's eyes glowed gold as she tried to shift but couldn't seem to complete the act. Perhaps being too close to the doorway between worlds prevented her. Darrien suspected as much. He could feel the beast inside him stirring, but lethargic as if drugged. The portal required energy and it interfered with the magic of a shifter's change.

Isa tried again to break free from his hold, but he wouldn't allow her to escape. He increased his grip on her. She winced and threw him a lethal glare filled with bitterness.

"You will face Spiro," he told her. "No more running." All at once, she stopped struggling, but he didn't trust how easily she stilled her attempts to flee.

She lifted her chin and narrowed her eyes on Spiro. "Callista always hated me. It is no wonder her spirit claimed I was the one at fault," she said with a hard cold voice, but her next words were spoken as if the memory proved too painful to recall. "That day...I came calling, only to speak to Darrien, but he was not at home. Callista invited me in with the pretense that she wanted us to be friends, but in truth she accused me of trying to steal Darrien away. It simply was not true." She paused for a theatrical affect before continuing her tale. "We had words and truly I tried to leave, but she would not allow it. She came after me with a dagger." She took a ragged breath and closed her eyes.

Darrien lifted his brows in astonishment when a single tear slid down her cheek.

"Her death was but an accident," she murmured. Her tear-filled eyes opened, and she brushed her hand over her face. "I had to defend myself." She sniffled and her hand fell to her chest, right where her heart lay beneath. Indeed, she did look contrite over the tragic event.

"O.M.G!" Calli said, drawing everyone's attention. "You aren't going to believe that load of crap?" She pointed to Isa. "She's about as innocent as a…a…fox in a chicken coop."

"Silence." Charon's voice boomed. "Do not speak out of turn."

"Truly, we should listen to her," Darrien said. "She is Callista reincarnated."

Spiro shifted his weight in the boat, taking steps closer and nearly capsizing them, but Charon was quick with his pole and steadied the craft. "Do not move, Spiro. Do you wish to tumble us into the river? Rest assured, only one of us will survive such a dunking," he said the last with meaning.

Spiro stilled his movements, but his eyes did not leave Calli. "It is you, my daughter." From his side of the portal, he would be able to see her soul as clearly as if she wore it upon her sleeve.

"It does not matter," Charon said. "A reincarnated soul does not recall his or her past life with accuracy. The soul is reborn to have a fresh start, to live and love again. A past life would only alter the destiny." He pinned his gaze on Calli. "Am I correct? Do you remember the altercation with Isa?"

"Uh…no, but—"

Charon held up his hand to halt her words. "Say no more."

"She may not remember," Darrien began, "but Charon, you can tell if Isa speaks the truth or not. I pray you will use your gift and see for yourself what lies Isa has spun this night." He would have this settled. He would have Callista's death finally avenged and justice served for the annihilation of his tribes. He had heard the stories about the souls crossing over to the other side, and how they had to literally bare their souls so Charon could deliver them to the respected level of Hades each of them deserved. He prayed there had been some truth to it, so the ferryman would know of Isa's deceit.

Charon tilted his head as he peered at Isa, his eyes hard and inscrutable. He lifted the pole, pulling it out of the river before he reached across the veil and offered it to Isa. "You will grip the end where the water still shimmers. Then plead your innocence. Let me see it shine from your eyes, Isa from the gryphon clans of Andros."

Isa threw Darrien a murderous look.

"Do what he asks," Darrien goaded her. "If you're innocent you have nothing to fear."

Her nostril's flared, but she turned away and stepped forward to clasp the end of the pole. The water glistened and slithered like a snake. It slid around her hand, fitting it like a glove and molding it to the pole, making it impossible for her to let go.

She took a deep breath then spoke loud and clear, "I defend my honor. I am not responsible for Callista's death. I—" Isa words stuck and choked her. She grabbed her throat with her free hand as water poured from her mouth.

Darrien frowned and took a step toward her, but Charon held up his hand. "Do not interfere," he warned.

Isa coughed until she could once again draw a breath. Her eyes bulged wide, and she didn't appear as confident as she had a moment ago.

"Every time you do not tell the truth," Charon said and waited for Isa to clear her throat once more. "You will choke on the water from the river, as the damned choke on the foul liquid for eternity."

For the first time, Darrien witnessed real fear in Isa's gaze. She wouldn't be able to spin a tale in her favor when Charon's eyes bore down on her in such a way. He controlled the water from the Styx, and he commanded it to sense if she spoke the truth or not. Drowning where she stood, obviously didn't appeal to her.

She stammered as she tried to think of something to save her life. "Callista was not one of us," she whined. "She was not a gryphon. She couldn't be of our tribe. I…" She stood straight and pursed her lips, realizing no matter what she said now, it would only condemn her further.

Darrien almost felt sorry for her…almost. She'd been blinded by hatred and prejudice all her life, and with each passing year it had blackened her soul until no pure light could seep through. He glanced at Spiro. "Isa threatens Callista again in this time and place where her soul has found a new life." He turned toward Calli and motioned for her to step forward, hoping she still trusted him. When he met her eyes, he witnessed a mixture of tenderness and determination within those green depths. How he loved his little thief. She never doubted him, and her sure steps brought her to his side, trusting him as she had when she lived her life as Callista.

Spiro's features softened as he gazed upon his daughter. "Callista." His voice was a hoarse whisper.

Calli remained quiet beside Darrien, pressing closer to his side. She trusted him and would allow Spiro his moment, even if she didn't wholeheartedly believe she was this man's daughter reincarnated.

Spiro leveled his gaze on Isa then, his eyes narrowing to slits. His whole demeanor changed as he stared at his daughter's murderer. "I demand justice be served for the death of my daughter."

"No, please, do not do this," Isa pleaded with Darrien. Terror of what awaited her shone bright in her eyes. She reached for him, but he would not take her hand. "I found the stone for you," she scrambled for words to save her life. "I…I found Callista and sent her to the museum. You would have never found her otherwise."

All she claimed was true, but it didn't change the fact Isa proved a threat he could ill afford if he were to keep Calli safe.

"Without the stone, you couldn't have this audience with Spiro," she told him. "He can release you from your punishment. Ask him. Go on. Do it."

"No, I accept my punishment as long as you are not here to threaten my beloved." He turned toward Charon then. "Isa has cheated death long enough." He fished a coin from his pocket and tossed it to the ferryman. "For a safe crossing, so she may be judged."

Isa tried one last attempt to escape. She managed to shift part way and drove her talons into the pole. A screech pierced the night as if the souls of the Styx felt the lash. Isa broke free and scrambled away from the veil, half crawling and half running.

Darrien attempted to go after her, but Charon's reflexes were quicker. He reached down and dipped his hand into the river. When he stood, he flung the water, transforming it into a lasso. He whipped it out and around Isa's waist, and he yanked back on the cord. She flew back with her hands outstretched, trying to grab anything to stop her flight. At the doorway, she gripped the edges, her knuckles turning white.

"Help me, Darrien." She met his gaze. She appeared vulnerable and tears glistened in her eyes. True tears and not fabricated ones meant to deceive. He turned away, but not before he witnessed the betrayal in her eyes.

Charon yanked on the cord again and Isa lost her hold. She fell through the doorway and landed on the bottom of the boat at Charon's feet. The lasso wound tightly around her arms like steel, making escape impossible.

"I curse you, Darrien," Isa spat. "I—"

With a flick of his wrist, Charon silenced her. Her lips moved, but no sound escaped. The ferryman then turned toward Darrien. "The retched soul will be judged for what she's done, and justice will be served. Is this all you demand from us, Darrien?"

"Nay, it is not. Isa possesses a ring. She stole it from a wizard and has used it against him and most likely others who were unfortunate enough to cross her path. May we have the ring so we may find out if the curses she exacted can be reversed?"

"And what will you give me in exchange?" Charon challenged.

Darrien had been prepared to barter. He held up Hecate's Stone. "This. I will give you the stone for the ring."

Charon seemed to consider the trade before he

nodded. "Agreed." With the bargain made, Darrien tossed Charon the stone. Charon then turned his attention on Isa, who tried to scoot away. He shook his head and crouched down beside her. His hand snaked out and held her firmly in place. He easily slipped the ring off her finger despite her struggles. He pushed Isa against the side of the boat as he stood. His fingers held the ring up to inspect with a careful eye. "It is an old ring, fashioned for the wearer to possess its power. I would look for the Wizards' Codex, a book containing rituals and spells. You should be able to unlock the ring's properties with it." He tossed the ring to Darrien. "I do not have to warn you of the consequences if the ring is used to harm others. This item was meant to assist. Most likely worn by a wizard sent to protect a kingdom."

"We only wish to undo what Isa has done."

"So be it," Charon said. "We will now depart on our—"

"Wait!" Calli interrupted and glanced at Darrien. "The curse," she said to him, but then addressed Spiro not Charon. "You can't leave Darrien cursed and chained to the museum. He was innocent," she pleaded. "Hasn't he suffered enough? Please, lift the spell."

Spiro simply shook his head, his eyes hauntingly filled with sadness and pity, too. "I am but a spirit, Callista, my daughter. I cannot harm or help those in the life beyond this door. I am deeply sorry." He shifted his gaze to Darrien. "If you wish for your torment to end, come with us. You'll be released from the curse as soon as you step past the threshold." He held out his hand as if he would assist him into the boat.

Charon nodded in agreement. "The cursed are

freed once they cross the barrier to the underworld. If you come with us, I assure you Elysium awaits your arrival, Darrien of old. It is where all champions go upon their death."

Calli turned to stare at Darrien, tears pooling in her eyes and making the green glisten like precious jewels. "Death is the only way you can find freedom?" she asked. "No, that can't be right." She shook her head in denial. "This can't be all we can do. I... Oh God... I don't want you to go. It's so unfair." Her eyes were wide and frightened within the pale frame of her face.

Her emotions washed over him in waves, desperation being among them. She didn't want him to go. In truth, he didn't want to leave her. With Hecate's Stone, he had believed there would be a chance for them, but all hope was dashed with Spiro's words. Cursed and tied to the museum, he could not offer her a future when he had none to give. Better he leave this world, so she could find another. If he remained, he would chain her to his destiny. He could see it in her eyes. She would stay with him. What life would that be? No, he could not allow her to make such a sacrifice.

"Darrien?" She must have sensed him withdrawing from her. In desperation, she reached for his hand, her touch so warm and true.

He raised her hand to his lips and placed a kiss. He then lowered her hand once more but didn't let her go. Tears glistened in her eyes. He had not had anyone care enough to cry for him in such a long time, his heart swelled to be so loved. "In another life, we were happy," he told her. "I see Callista in you, but you are also Calli, a sweet woman who cared enough to help me. Without your assistance, I could not have found peace."

Her breath caught in her throat. "No. Don't you do this. Dammit, you made me care about you." She was fishing for anything to make him stay. Humans were never ready to let the living go, even if it were for the best. "What about your other half?" she asked. "I didn't even have a chance to say goodbye. He doesn't know we did it. He doesn't know we stopped Isa."

He gave her a whisper of a smile. "He knows. He is a part of me." He placed a hand on his chest. He'd avenged Callista's death, and he insured Calli would be safe to live out her life without the fear of Isa hunting her down. In his mind's eye, he could see the life Calli had yet to live, and there was no room for him in it.

Her eyes darkened with anger, and she yanked her hand free. She turned toward Charon again. "I can't accept this. It can't be all you can do." She waved her hand at him accusingly. "You're powerful. You can see into a person's soul and find them wanting or not. You can transform the water to do your bidding. You can do something that will break the curse, right?"

"Calli?" Darrien stepped toward her, wanting to stop her before she angered Charon, but she waved him away and moved out of reach.

"Don't," she warned. "I want him to answer me." She pointed to Charon behind her, but kept her eyes locked on Darrien.

"The curse cannot be broken in the sense you would prefer," Charon finally spoke up, but not with anger as Darrien had feared. "However," the ferryman continued, "there may be another solution, a way to alter it." He then addressed only Darrien, "The curse severed your essence to a point. The human side and your shifter side hang onto each other by a mere thread."

Of this, Darrien understood all too clearly, now that Calli had shown him how the curse worked. He suspected such a rift but believed the more human side had simply been repressed due to the curse. With the video Calli supplied, he witnessed the separation. "Go on," he told Charon, hopeful for a solution.

"I cannot repair the rift, but I can sever the tie completely, and thus the curse will be broken."

"But?" Calli asked, suspicion lacing her one word. "There's always a stipulation. What is it? What price must Darrien pay for this service?"

Charon for once lost his indifference, his features revealing sorrow. "One of the essences will have to cross over to this side. Only one can continue to live. It will allow the one part of the soul to heal and thrive as if reborn."

"So either I live, or my daytime self does," Darrien stated.

"You understand correctly," Charon said. "It will be your choice, of course." He nodded then stood there patiently, awaiting his decision.

Darrien turned toward Calli. Which of his essences would she want? Which one could offer her protection and passion too? She deserved to be loved, completely.

She took the steps separating them. Her hand reached for him, and he clasped it to his heart. "Oh, Darrien, it is not a solution if you lose part of yourself." She choked back a sob.

"I have lived a long time, longer than any gryphon should," he said. "Everyone should love and be loved, sweet Calli. I was lucky to experience both." With his free hand, he wiped away a tear from her cheek. Gryphons loved forever. It was in their nature. He cherished Callista with all his heart, but she was gone. Calli could never be her completely, and he didn't begrudge her. She deserved a fresh start. Perhaps he could have one with a human existence, where there would be no past to haunt him.

He leaned down and kissed her, a tender kiss goodbye. He opened her hand and placed the wizard's ring in her palm. "You know what to do with this." Then he released her and turned to face Charon. "I choose the human side to stay."

"What are you doing? We can find another way." Calli's voiced hitched with panic, but he could not comfort her.

"Do it now." Darrien met Charon's gaze and the ferryman reached across the veil and placed the pole on his shoulder. He spoke the words of old like a graceful chant. The water from the river seeped into him, both cool and startling as it raced through his veins at an alarming rate. Then an excruciating pain ripped through him, tearing him apart, consuming him until he could no longer see what stood in front of him. He could no longer hear Calli's cries or Charon's words. For a space of time, everything ceased to be.

Chapter Twenty-Two

Calli watched in horror while Darrien withered in pain. She could do nothing to help him. A burst of light consumed him, so bright she had to cover her eyes, but then the illumination dimmed then ebbed away completely. She glanced where Darrien had once stood. Now both his personas were there. One wore black-rimmed glasses, a cardigan, and slacks—nerdy Darrien. The other, the gryphon shifter, strong and true, and with eyes mimicking the eerie glow like how the gryphon's eyes glimmered. Both circled as if sizing up the other for their worth.

In such a short time, she'd come to care for both of them. No matter what was decided, she would mourn the loss of one of them. She could feel sorry for herself, but nothing could compare to what Darrien would have to give up.

Darrien of old spoke, his voiced deep with purpose. "Keep her safe," he told his other half as he glanced at Calli. "And love her with all your heart."

His human counterpart appeared confused, awe-struck to be face to face with his bolder self. He too glanced at Calli. He must have sensed the urgency of the words and the need to take them seriously. He straightened his shoulders and faced his other half once more. "You have my word."

Ancient Darrien turned away and strode toward the veil, not pausing as he stepped through the doorway and into the boat, his decision made.

Calli came to stand beside the Darrien who'd been left in her world and reached for his hand. He laced his fingers through hers and gave her hand a quick squeeze.

Spiro had remained silent until now. When he spoke, his surprise rang through in his words. "You truly care for him, my sweet daughter," he said, not as a question but as an observation.

Calli sighed and straightened her back. "I do care for him."

"Ah…he cares for you too," Spiro said with a heavy sigh. "I cannot fault such affections."

"I don't remember my time with Darrien as Callista," Calli said and glanced at the other Darrien in the boat. Her heart ached for him. "I wanted to see Darrien whole, not split like this."

Spiro's lips curved slightly and not without sympathy. "I can see the soul which stands beside you. It pulses like a heartbeat when he touches you. It will be enough, I believe."

"Calli, my sweet thief who stole my heart," the Darrien from the boat addressed her. "Do not fret. There is a second opportunity for happiness." He glanced at his other half. "All I ask is you give him a chance to win your heart. We have all paid long enough for Isa's treachery, and it is time to forgive and let the past go." Then he glanced at Isa, who stared wide-eyed as she continued to try and break the bonds holding her.

Calli followed his line of vision. She pitied Isa as she would a rabid animal in need of being put down. Something happened to her, and she couldn't be reasoned with any longer. She had lost all sense of honor and compassion for others. Isa couldn't be saved and must meet her fate, long denied.

She glanced at the man who held her hand, her nerdy Darrien with his quick wit and love for tea. He gazed at her with longing. A good man, courageous despite his claims to the contrary, one she could fall for. Who was she kidding? She was halfway there already. Perhaps her destiny would prove to be the future with him.

"What do you say, Darrien?" she asked the man beside her. "Should I stick around for a while?"

His lips curved. "I would be most pleased."

"So be it," Charon said. "The night is done and the door between the veils must close."

"Goodbye, my sweet daughter," Spiro called to Calli. "May you live long with joy in your heart."

Charon leaned down and released the ropes tied to the pillar. As the boat floated away, the winds picked up around Calli and Darrien on their side of the realm. Then the door between the worlds rippled like the river, blurring what lay beyond before ebbing away into nothing.

The wind ceased whipping around them just as suddenly as it had picked up, and for a moment, the silence proved almost as deafening as the roaring wind. Calli sighed long and hard as she tried to come to terms with what transpired. It might take her a lifetime.

She gave Darrien a sideward glance with a tilt of her head. His fingers massaged his chest right over the area where the bullet would have entered, but his cardigan showed no signs of being damaged—as if it had mended along with his wound. She could only imagine the magic of the shift was responsible for the transformation on both accounts. Yet, his essence must still feel where he'd been shot. "Does the wound hurt?"

"What do you mean?" His brow furrowed then he must have realized what he was doing and glanced at where his hand rested. "The skin feels prickly."

She frowned and wondered why he would have discomfort if he'd been healed. She wanted to make sure he was truly okay. "May I?" she motioned with a nod of her head. "Will you let me take a look?"

He lowered his hand. "Sure."

As she unbuttoned his shirt, she noticed his skin flushed at her touch. As endearing as that was, she remained concerned about his well-being. She needed to see if he was still injured. She pulled the shirt and cardigan away, revealing what lay beneath. Her breath caught in her throat as she stared at his chest in disbelief, something moved beneath the skin, the movement continuing down his arm. Darrien rolled up his sleeve in haste. The thing beneath the skin settled at his forearm, the skin darkening as if ink had been applied to form the image that appeared as it etched.

"What is it?" he voiced with worry and glanced at his limb as if he would like to cast it away. "Blimey, is that a tattoo?" he answered his own question and lowered his glasses to peer at the design as if he couldn't trust the magnification of his prescription lens.

"Apparently." Her fingers smoothed over the intricate gryphon drawn with golden wings. The wings gleamed brighter as her hand brushed over them. "Did it hurt?" she asked and met his eyes.

"No. It feels warm, though not unpleasantly so." He covered her hand with his. "A parting gift from Charon, I suppose. In memory of the shifter."

She nodded with a hint of a smile. "You are part of

the gryphon. You always have been." She stood on her tippy toes and kissed his cheek.

But when his gaze met hers, it seemed he wanted so much more. He cradled her head as he claimed her lips. The invisible threads binding their souls pulled tighter, and electricity sparked between them. She inhaled sharply and pulled away to stare at him.

"You felt it too?" he asked.

"Yes." Longing shone in his golden-brown depths, and she knew her eyes must mirror the same desires.

"I want you, Calli. I won't deny it, but I want to take this, whatever this is, at a slower pace. I am not sure what I can offer you when I have never had a place in this world…until now."

He had so much to offer, but she understood what he meant. His life up until now had been fabricated, a lie with false memories. He needed to find his footing and a purpose.

"Agreed. We will see where our new friendship takes us."

"Friends?" He said with a long sigh. "Isn't that a kiss of death to a relationship?"

She straightened his shirt and cardigan over his shoulder but didn't lower the sleeve to cover the gryphon design. "No, it's the beginning of a relationship with the hopes of so much more to come."

Chapter Twenty-Three

Calli and Darrien drove to the hotel in her sedan, while she filled him in on all that had transpired—at least the parts that led up to his beastie side making a deal with Charon. Too tired to do more than clean up and cuddle on the bed, then finally too exhausted for anything else, they snuggled close and managed a few hours of shuteye. It seemed natural to have him at her back with his arm draped around her possessively with his warmth cloaking her, making her feel safe.

Later, when they finally woke, Darrien took his shower first. After her turn in the bathroom, Calli felt more alive than she had in a long time. Rested but hungry, she and Darrien agreed to stop for breakfast then drive back to the museum.

"We will face the new day together. Yeah?"

"Absolutely." Calli agreed and offered to drive. "Get in the car. I don't know about you, but I have a million questions. We can talk on the way to the museum."

After picking up groceries on the way, they went over the endless questions each of them had regarding Darrien's new life.

"With the curse broken, you still have to exist in this world," Calli reminded him. "That requires paperwork, legal documents, and who knows what else? I'll call my cousin."

Once they got to the museum, Calli made a few calls, one to Mick in New Orleans. A few minutes later, she smiled at Darrien and clicked off the call. "My cousin has all the connections to get the documents you'll need to establish a new identity."

He'd be set as far as documents went, but he still needed a job—preferably one that paid. Calli brewed a pot of coffee as she talked.

"I'm worried. There's still the matter of the museum. It can't be left unattended, and I have a hunch the head honchos who brought in the cursed items won't allow them to go unprotected. You," she pointed at him, "probably won't be able to abandon them."

She offered a cup of coffee to Darrien while he sat at his desk, deep in thought. Barely glancing her way, he frowned as he took the mug from her. After taking a generous sip, he placed it down in front of him.

"What are you thinking about?" she asked.

"You kissed...? You know. Him?" Darrien whispered the last word as his fingers rubbed his arm where the tattoo lay. He still frowned, but seemed to realize what he was doing and dropped his hand.

"I don't believe he can hear you," she told him with a smile then sipped her coffee. He'd lived through a fantastic ordeal, and yet he worried if she'd kissed his other half. It was so very human of him, so much a guy thing, and so very, very normal.

Darrien slid his chair back and stood, frowning with displeasure. "You did kiss him," he answered his own question with certainty. "Does he kiss better than I do?" He strode over to her.

She chuckled now. This was just too humorous for words. "You're jealous?"

He pushed his glasses back on the bridge of his nose, making him look all Clark Kent kind of sexy. Really, the superhero alter ego couldn't downplay his allure behind a pair of glasses and Darrien couldn't either.

"Well, yeah. I am," he told her. "There I said it. I'm pea-green with jealousy."

She placed her coffee cup next to his on the desk. "You were him and he was you, remember? So if I kissed your alter ego, I was still kissing you." He didn't look at all convinced. She removed his glasses and ruffled his hair before she lazily rested her forearms on his shoulders. "I'm crazy in 'like' with you, Darrien Andros," she said, but he wouldn't look at her. "Every last inch of you—shifter, man, even when you're the sexy nerd with black-rimmed glasses." She smiled when his gaze riveted to hers. "Thought that would get your attention."

"You think I'm sexy?" His voice cracked, endearing him to her more.

"I said 'all of you'." She cupped his face, encouraging him to lower his head so she could kiss the tip of his nose. She could feel him relax beneath her touch. His arms went around her, and he pulled her flush against him. Boy, did she love the way it felt to be in his arms.

"So you're crazy 'in like' with me?" he asked, using her words.

"Uh-huh, but what about you?"

"What do you mean?" He frowned. "Of course, I like you."

"Good. You had me worried for a moment," she told him in good humor as she placed his glasses back on the bridge of his nose. She brushed his shoulder with a swipe of her hand as if she were removing lint. Then she rested her hand there. "Do you think we'd make a good team?"

"A good team for what?"

"You know, like maybe we could work together. Of course, we'll have to have a chat with whoever is in charge of delivering the items to the museum."

"The Guards of Judgment," he reminded her. "They are the Nephilim dedicated to keeping the human realm safe from those who wish to harm it."

He sounded like a commercial endorsement for this elite group of Nephilim. "They take care of all the preternatural business?" she asked.

He nodded with a heavy sigh. "They usually contact me. I do have a phone number. You know, in case of an emergency."

"Really? Fallen Angels... I mean the Nephilim have phones?"

He lifted his shoulders in a shrug. "Cursed curators apparently do also."

"So they do." She smiled. "We should call them. Present our plans." She stared at the ring on her finger. It was the one Isa used against her and turned her to stone. Seemed harmless in the light of day, but she knew the magic it held and the effects this piece of jewelry could invoke.

She'd been to Isa's office. There had been a wizard and an angel statue there. It didn't take much imagination on her part to suspect they'd both been flesh and blood at one time. It would explain the eerie feeling she had felt about them, the same feeling she had when she laid eyes on the gryphon statue for the first time. They were frozen, but there was still a soul trapped inside. Energy never truly died, and it seemed it couldn't be completely encased in stone either.

"Surely, the Nephilim would like to know the fate of their fellow brethren," she said. "Maybe they'll be able to reverse the curse. We have the wizard's ring. We'll offer it to them in good faith, and with the hope they'll work with us in return. Pay us to recover cursed items and keep them safe here at the museum." She didn't run a recovery business for free. She and her dad had always worked well together, and she missed him, missed their talks and their late nights when they would plan their next heist. Her hand went to her necklace, the one her dad had given to her, a stone to keep a thief safe. Maybe it had done its job after all.

"So, we'll be like superheroes from a comic book," Darrien said. "Hunting down cursed artifacts and saving the world from destruction."

He really was a nerd, and God help her, she loved that most about him. "Sure, why not?"

"The Gryphon and His Thief," Darrien teased.

All superheroes had secret identities. She had her share of comic books stashed in her room back home.

"Has a good ring to it. Yeah?" he asked.

"Yeah." She tilted her head as he moved in for a kiss, but then he hesitated, pulling back slightly to meet her gaze.

"Just so you know," he told her, "I plan on kissing you until your toes curl."

Her lips slid into a broad grin. "I never doubted you wouldn't." His mouth finally found hers and went to work on his promise. Her hand rested on his forearm over the gryphon tattoo. The area warmed beneath her touch, and she could have sworn the wings fluttered as if the gryphon offered his approval.

Visit the author at her website:

http://www.kmnbooks.com
Blog: http://kmnbooks.blogspot.com
Gillian's Book Covers,
"Judge Your Book By Its Cover"
http://judgeyourbookbyitscover.blogspot.com
Facebook:
https://www.facebook.com/authorkarenmichellenutt
Twitter:
https://twitter.com/KMNbooks
Pinterest: http://pinterest.com/karenmnutt
Instagram: https://www.instagram.com/kmn_books
BookBub: https://www.bookbub.com/authors/karen-
michelle-nutt
GoodReads:
https://www.goodreads.com/karenmichellenutt
Linkedin:
https://www.linkedin.com/in/karenmichellenutt
YouTube:
https://www.youtube.com/user/kmnbooks
IMDb: https://tinyurl.com/yy27qubr

Thank you for purchasing
this publication of The Wild Rose Press, Inc.
For questions or more information
contact us at
info@thewildrosepress.com.
The Wild Rose Press, Inc.
www.thewildrosepress.com